THE BONE CUTTERS

Renee S. DeCamillis

Encyclopocalypse Publications
www.encyclopocalypse.com

ACKNOWLEDGMENTS

Thank you to The Odd Stones Alliance--Dave, Shawna, Cecilia, Karen, Olivia, & Brigitte—for their continued support and valued advice.

A very special thank you goes to Jesse and Sandro for everything, always, with much love.

To Mom, Patricia A. DiPaolo Richards Young (1946-2013), the one who always believed in me, the one who knew I was a writer before I knew it myself. This is for you, Mom.

THE
BONE
CUTTERS

CHAPTER 1

A SUDDEN KNOCK on the doorframe of my room startles me. The black marker in my hand streaks across my sketch pad.

I'm not allowed to have a pencil—I might use it as a weapon.

Before I turn toward the door, my hand moves up to my head and starts scratching.

"Come on. It's time for group. You're late. Let's go." A redheaded nurse, toe tapping rhythmically on the linoleum, calls into my closet-with-a-bed. The pastel colored butterfly print scrubs she's wearing, along with that thick shimmering hair, scream Mary Poppins. If she starts singing, I'm going to vomit.

Mind foggy, I hesitate before I say, "I haven't been assigned a counseling group yet." My fingers scratch harder. I can feel the fuzz of hair growing back on my bald spot. I don't want to go to *any* group.

"Oh, no worries, dear. I know *exactly* whose hands to put you in." I'm not sure how to read the smile she gives me. Then she looks at the clipboard in her hand. She happily huffs, if that's even possible, and rolls her eyes. But that creepy smile remains. "You haven't had your meds. *Why* haven't you had your meds?" Not waiting for my answer, she says, "No worries. I'll fix that. Let's go, dear." She wills me out into the hall with a wave of her hand, almost like a puppeteer. I can feel the pull.

Dear? And that smile—I think *she* took my meds.

After a quick stop at the nurse's station, a plop of meds and water into my mouth, the redheaded nurse— Nurse Hatchet is what the tag on her lanyard reads— ushers me through the first door we come to that has a group of patients gathered inside. The door clicks shut behind me. I reach under my tongue, pocket my meds. My hand involuntarily starts scratching my head, again. I'm about to turn and flee, until every face in the circle of people whips toward me. My eyes immediately look away. I look down at the black and white checkered floor. I shove my shaky hands into the pockets of my jeans. With my sneakered-foot, I push an empty plastic chair toward the group of patients.

I enter the circle.

I have no idea if I'm in the right group. It's only my second day here. Feeling all eyes on me, I can't force myself to look up, to look anyone in the face.

Silence.

Shuffling.

A cough.

A man starts talking.

A weight lifts off from me.

The attention is now on someone else.

After a couple minutes of what I assume is someone's psycho-babble, it feels safe to look up from the floor. His words —I can't hear any of them. The vice that repeatedly squeezes on my head and chest has always caused a malfunction with my hearing, ever since I was a child. With the arrival of my teen years, it never got any better—which is how I've ended up where I am.

Institutionalized.

A new voice sounds out. I turn toward the sound.

A skeletal-thin man speaks with passion of an insatiable hunger. His voice sounds strained, scraping and clawing its way out of his mouth, stumbling past his dry cracked lips. His eyes scream pain, empty and hollow, drained of what may have been behind those doors before.

With every syllable he utters, I can't stop staring at his neck. With every bob of his Adam's apple, I'm fascinated, mesmerized. With every bob of his Adam's apple it slithers around the base of his neck.

The scar.

The size of a mutant slug—fat and glistening— with a thickness five times my thumb's width.

How did it get there? What is it from?

Does it hurt? Itch? Throb?

Does he ever, sometimes, forget that it's there?

These questions shoot through my mind in rapid succession —as I stare.

I can't make sense of the scarred man's words. My questions are too loud. Too many. And I can't stop staring.

I need to hear his words.

I force myself to listen. Now I can't not listen. I can't un-hear the insanity, the desperation. His story is permanently etched into my brain.

"I reopen it when I need to re-up." The man speaks with a gravelly voice. The slug writhes and slithers with every word. "I scrape a good amount with each incision. The more I chisel and collect, the less often I need to slice open the wound again. I stitch it. Let it scab over. Let the scab loosen and fall away before my supply runs out."

Supply?

Supply of what?

From the opposite side of the circle a woman picks up where the scarred man's words fade away. The sound of her voice jars my attention away from the slug. Her words drag and drone and trip across the open hollow of the circle, landing in my disbelieving-ears. "Then it starts all over again. The self-surgery. The extraction."

The woman is scarred, too. Not her neck. Her upper arm. It snakes along the outside of her bicep. It starts at her elbow and slithers up onto her shoulder. Thicker than the man's slug. And a lot longer. Snake-girl. "It hurts like Hell, but it's free. Music to a user's ears—free high."

Free high?

The term stuns me to stone, heavy and unmoving.

I don't want to hear anymore.

My eyes start scanning the circle of people. Every one of them is scarred. All in a different location on their bodies.

Cutters.

How did I not notice this defining detail when I first entered into this circle?

"Users"—junkies.

The wrong group for me.

But I can't speak up. I can barely breathe. I want to slip away, unnoticed, but I can't even move. My nerves have tied me to the hard plastic chair.

A few moments pass. Maybe many moments. I don't know. Someone is talking. My ears don't hear anything but my frantic garbled thoughts of how I can flee undetected. I can't even decipher what's sounding in my head. There might be a good idea in the chaos of my mind, but I can't lasso one out.

A strand of hair falls in my face. It starts tickling my nose. I force my hand to tuck my hair behind my ear. My hands are wet, sweaty. I slowly rest my hand on my knee. Now my knee is bouncing. I can't stop the involuntary motions.

Shaking.

Bouncing.

Shaking.

Bouncing.

Sweat. Sweat. Sweat.

"Never let them see you sweat."

Too late.

The sweat is causing wisps of my hair to stick to my forehead. Then I notice the blood—under my fingernails. I curl my fingers under. Does anyone notice? If not the blood, all of them must see my bald spot by now.

The counselor hasn't said a word. I don't even know which one *is* the counselor.

Every *one* of them is scarred.

A counselor with first-hand experience, I guess.

They say that's the best kind, most respected by patients, especially addicts.

Who are *they* anyway?

A voice. Someone is talking. Louder now. Is it a different person? Or the same? I don't know. At this point nothing is making sense.

A garbled voice echoes in my head. By the sounds of it, the voice is traveling through a tunnel before it reaches my ears. Is it a man or a woman? I don't know. I can't even make out any of the words. It's as though all the words are jumbled together, overlapping, tossed together like a salad. I can't look to see who's talking. They'll see the confusion plastered on my face. They'll know I don't belong. They'll think I'm judging them.

Never judge. I don't know where they've traveled.

Their shoes don't fit me.

I can't focus on the voice anymore. It's too maddening. I stare, instead, at the scars.

The slug. The snake.

I can't take it anymore. If I can't make myself leave, I need to know . . .

I don't want to know, but questions fly, like hurricane winds, out of my mouth before I can rein them back. The loud person is still talking when I blurt out, "You get *high* by carving into your own body? *All* of you?" I scan the circle, addressing the group. My eyes can't focus on any one face. Instead, my eyes dart back and forth and round and round from person to person. They all nod in unison. As soon as people turn toward me, I feel the flames reddening my cheeks. I don't see their eyes on me. I feel them. "How? I don't understand," my voice croaks, barely letting the words slip out. It feels like a snake is wrapped around *my* throat, constricting.

Sweat drips faster. My bloody fingers start scratching the peach fuzz again. Why can't I leave it alone, let the hair grow back, look normal again?

The thought makes me scratch harder.

My eyes accidentally fall on a husky tattooed man in camouflage shorts. His drug-serpent slithers along his shin. Very fitting with his Medusa tattoo. The artist worked it into her snake-hair, almost undetectable as a scar—

until I'd realized this is a group of cutters. Not your typical cutters. They cut to get high. Somehow. Some way. A high follows every cut.

I don't get it.

The Medusa Man reluctantly, almost painfully, speaks up. It's as though my eyes pushed him to talk. The veins in his neck are bulging out, a network of rivers. Every word that emerges from him looks, and sounds, like a weightlifting challenge to haul up from his vocal chords out into the audible world. The result—the voice of a pre-pubescent boy coming from a man. "It's in the bones. Everyone's bones. His." He nods toward Slug Man. "Hers." He nods toward Snake Girl. "Even yours." He looks, unblinking, straight into my stinging eyes.

The shock must be painted on my face.

His eyes widen and he nods. "Yes, even *your* bones." I shake my head, rub my eyes. The sweat stings.

Slug Man—he acts as the spokesman for the group. "You look confused. Let me explain—Once we slice ourselves open and get down to the bone, we chisel and scrape bone dust into little baggies, onto tinfoil— whatever the choice. It's like heroin, but all natural. We can cook it and inject it. We can smoke it. Snort it. Best of all—it's free."

"Best of all?" I cringe. My stomach turns. My skin itches, like spiders are crawling all over me. Scratching my head, my hair slicks back as though it hasn't been washed in days. Blood, warm and slick, starts dripping down my forehead.

My knee is bouncing faster. It won't stop.

No judgment. No judgment. No judgment.

Now it's time for my burning question—"How the Hell did all of you find out about this . . . this drug-like substance in our bones?"

Slug Man speaks through his gap-toothed grin. "From my work at the crematorium."

Each cutter, each addict, starts stating how they made their discovery. All eyes are on me as they speak. I can't force myself to look directly at any of them. I can't understand what any one of them is saying. They're all speaking at once. They're all staring at me. And they're all getting closer.

My eyes dart around the circle, around the room. The groups' voices are getting louder as they're all getting closer to me. Metal chair legs squeak and scrape across linoleum. I scan the room for the door. I'm disoriented. Displaced. I can't remember which side of the room I came in through.

Scanning.

Scanning.

There it is. The door. It's behind me.

Just as I'm able to peel my sweat-drenched back off from the chair and unglue my ass from the unforgiving hard plastic seat, I notice, as I start to stand, that I'm now surrounded. I'm in the middle.

In the center of the circle of addicts. The cutters.

All eyes on me.

I take a deep breath. My return-breath trips and stumbles up my throat and gets lodged there.

What do I do? What can I say?

All eyes on me. Big, bulging, hungry eyes. Craving eyes.

Staring.

Judging.

Wanting.

Staring.

Judging.

Wanting.

My skin crawls. My hand scratches. More blood drips.

The more I bleed the wider the users' eyes grow. I can't breathe.

I can't breathe.

I can't fucking breathe!

The door. I see it. I stare at it. It's close at first. But the longer I stare, the farther and farther away it moves.

Feet frozen to the floor like a tongue on an icy flagpole, I'm unable to move.

The room starts spinning. My head is going to burst.

Where's my breath? I can't find my breath!

I have to move. I need to leave. How can I get the fuck out?

I see the door. It's so far away. I don't think I can make it. I don't know if I can even make myself move. Then I feel a breath. A breath not my own. It's blowing hot against my neck.

I turn. A hand reaches for me. I flinch, but not fast enough. A long, rough finger slides across my forehead then quickly pulls away.

Snake-girl. She licks her finger. "Mmm . . . Fresh. I bet I can get to your bones fast, you skinny little ball of nerves. Won't hurt me one bit." She leans toward me and sniffs my sopping hair, what's left of it.

That's it. I can't fucking take it anymore! Somehow, some way, I find the strength to move. With a crash and a clatter, I bolt.

CHAPTER 2

KICKING, thrashing my arms, I'm trying anything and everything just to get away, to get free. With every ounce of energy I exert, all it does is flail my body up and down and side to side in mid-air. Someone is holding each leg, each arm, and carrying me down the valium-blue hallway in quick jerking motions.

The four-point assist. More like the tackle-and-restrain-in-order-to-control method.

Who *wouldn't* freak out?

If you say you wouldn't, I say you're a liar.

I scream. I cry out. Echoes reverberate through the corridors. Patients are all gathering, whispering, pointing, laughing hysterically, pulling their hair, spitting on me. One skinny old man follows along beside us as I'm freaking out, poking me in the ribs repeatedly with a giant chewed up straw. My stomach and ribs are bare where my shirt is rising up. An orderly's assisting-hand is cupping and pinching the side of my breast.

This happens every time.

I swear only pervs work in the trenches of the mental health system, where they can get their cheap thrills and then deny it and get away with it—as they drive away in their old 90's Camaro, with their GED and their community college credit hours and their comb-over and wearing their sweat-stained wife-beater and blasting Whitesnake on their cassette player stereo—and as long they always make it back to punch the clock for their next shift, they'll have job security. For the mental patient isn't a reliable witness. The mental patient isn't a reliable anything.

Wait. Try that again:

The mental patient isn't an anything. The mental patient is a nothing, a nobody.

A loud clunky crash rings out. I wince. I see a clipboard flipping through the air. I see bottles of meds flying, then bouncing and rolling and tumbling across the black and white checkered linoleum floor. Some burst open, sending pills skittering everywhere. A shattering rainbow of psychotropics. A hail storm of mood stabilizers. Little plastic cups, a big pitcher of water, the clipboard with now sopping wet pages stuck to it. The medication cart.

My final kick stops that demonic device before it makes it through the half-door to the nurses' station. Intentional? Who's to say? It doesn't matter what *I* say. They won't believe any of it. I'm Blue-Papered. I'm mental. Crazy. Remember?

That's what *they* all tell me.

The four horsemen toss me through an open doorway. I hit the floor with a thud. My vision has turned blurry. The sweat stings my eyes. I grope around to find the bed. There is no bed. This isn't my assigned room.

It's the calm room. The take-a-break room. It's the mellow-out room. The seclusion room.

It's the fucking padded room!

The door slams shut. The lock clicks into place. I'm alone.

Alone in a room that's entirely white. Yeah, this is going to calm me down.

Oh, wait. I *do* get a window. One window. A little, square mesh-filled window three quarters of the way up the door. A window for voyeurs. The observation window.

All this just for trying to save my own life. I'm the violent one? I'm a harm to others?

I don't even want to be *around* other people, let alone *hurt* other people. I hate people. Their greedy, self-centered selves, with their total disregard for anyone's wellbeing other than their own. I can't even stand the stench of their judgmental thoughts. Their evil intentions reek like overflowing septic tanks of self- righteous entitlement.

Some might say I'm a misanthrope.

No.

I'm a realist. A survivalist. But violent?

No.

Maybe if I hadn't thrown my chair, and the two beside me, and knocked down those junkie-cutters like bowling pins, and then slammed open the Group Room door screaming to be saved from the demon addicts who want to inject my bone dust. Maybe. Maybe if that hadn't happened. Maybe. Maybe then I wouldn't get labeled "delusional". Maybe then my diagnosis wouldn't get tagged "with psychotic tendencies."

Maybe.

Maybe not.

No. No one believes *anything* I say. Don't forget—I came attached with a Blue Paper. Involuntary committal.

CHAPTER 3

I DON'T KNOW how long I've been sleeping, but I don't want to open my eyes. Sleep never lasts long enough. The smell of bleach fills my nostrils. My cheek is drool-soaked against my rubbery floor pillow. Rolling over to stretch and readjust my position, I accidentally open my eyes.

Damn it! I think they saw me.

I close my eyes again. Pretend I'm still sleeping.

Maybe by chance they didn't notice.

A few seconds tick by, then the door scrapes open. The friction of padding against padding stands my arm hairs on end. I shiver, though I'm sweating.

"I'm just here to change your dressings, and then you can go back to sleep. It'll just take a couple minutes, dear." My dry lips taste salty when I lick them. I was going to say something, but words don't come to mind. When I reach to wipe the sleep from the corners of my eyes, I see trails as my arm appears to move in slow motion. It looks like my hand is unnaturally far away from my face as it moves closer in pulses and waves. And heavy. Am I lifting a car or my fucking hand?

What damn Devil Dope did they give me this time?

A sedative? A tranquilizer? Probably both.

With all the man-made chemicals these places send through your mind and body, it's a wonder how anyone ever survives to see the outside world again. How anyone even remembers who they are or how to tie their own shoes. And the shrinks—the mind-scrambling mad scientists who think they're Gods—wonder why they keep seeing the same people get readmitted over and over again.

We're not patients, we're guinea pigs. Test subjects for the Devil doctors.

When my hand finally gets just about close enough to dig out the sleep boogers from my eyes, I see dried blood on my fingers. Then I remember the scratching. The blood on my forehead. Snake Girl, with her forked tongue licking her bloody fingers. Okay, maybe it wasn't forked. Then I notice dried blood trails coming down my hands from the red stained bandages on my forearms.

I forgot about that.

The pain was nonexistent, until seeing the bloody bandages. Now the cuts sting and throb and ache. Then Nurse Hatchet unwraps the bandage and peels off the gauze pad, yanking the sutures in the process.

"Ow! Shit. That hurts worse than slicing myself."

No response. She doesn't even look me in the face. The redheaded sadist just keeps doing her job, while whistling some chipper tune. And that creepy smile, it never wavers.

Wait. I recognize that tune. "Here I Go Again," Whitesnake.

What? How did she know I had recently been thinking of that band?

As the throbbing in my wounds intensifies, nausea gurgles in my gut. Though I was already sweaty, now skin juice is gathering in beads on my forehead. I feel them tickle and itch as they begin their rolling descent toward my temples. I squeeze my eyes shut, clench my jaw. Then the stomach contraction hits me.

I hate puking, but here it comes. The Barf Train can't be stopped once it starts chugging along, picking up speed as it rails up my throat.

I try sitting up, but I'm too heavy. I try rolling over away from the nurse, but when I yank the arm that's in her hands, she squeezes tight and pulls me closer.

Okay, smiley-creeper, if that's how you want to play. With one uncontrollable lurch, I hurl all over her legs, where she's been kneeling beside my head—safely out of kicking range. Her colorful butterfly-print scrubs aren't so Spring-pleasant anymore.

Who in their right mind would wear such attire in a psych ward anyway? Do you want some psycho flipping their lid when they think you're being eaten by one of nature's most delicate creatures? Seriously! You people are supposed to help alleviate your patients' symptoms, not exacerbate them.

Letting out a huff—with a smile—Nurse Hatchet drops my arm, bandage free with all its blood smeared cuts and crusty stitches, right into my puddle of liquidy gut chunks.

Yeah. You think that sounds disgusting? Try laying your arm in it. Feeling it on your skin. Smelling its pungent stench right beside your face. And I thought the bleach smell was unpleasant.

Fluttered away by vomit covered butterflies, and whistling cheerily again, the nurse pushes open the padded door, floats into the hallway, and calls for "Clean up in the quiet room. ASAP!"

I guess that means I have to sit up now. Why can't I just sleep forever?

In the corner adjacent to the door, I sit with my knees

hugged tight to my chest. My forearm is throbbing. I pull my sleeve down. A makeshift bandage. Well, actually, I just don't want to see my wounds—pain-filled reminders. With the scars that will no doubt stay behind, I guess I can count on them as constant reminders.

Lovely.

I foresee long sleeves forever in my future. Yes, I'm psychic.

Do you want to see what's down the road for you? That'll be seventy-five dollars for a thirty-minute session. Cash only.

A jarring metallic *squeak-grind-clunk* sound is echoing outside my cell. I hear it trailing down the linoleum hallway floor, getting closer and closer. As unnerving as it is at first, I start to notice a rhythm in the rolling of the metal wheels. I don't need to see it to know what it is.

As the mop bucket is pulling up right outside the door, I begin to notice the scuffing sound of the janitor's non-skid shoes. A rhythmic accompaniment to the bucket wheels. Much better than the soundless vacuum of this padded room when the door is shut. Non-sound—*that*'s disturbing.

Before he steps into my cell, I know it's a guy. I can tell by the walk. I hide my face in my knees. The strings from the hole in my jeans tickle my nose. I tolerate it. Well, actually, the tickle is better than the strain of sitting upright. My head feels so heavy. Lying it on my legs is like resting between weightlifting sets.

Plus, the idea of facing another person I don't know, it's unbearable. In this position, the janitor will get a clear view of my bald spot. But, at this point in the game, I don't have the energy to give a fuck.

Sitting as still as death, I hear the mop bucket *thud- clunk* up and over the door frame. The sound of the wheels muffle as it lands on the padded floor. (Yes, even the floor is padded. A lot of damage can come from a hard floor surface. Believe me. I know.) I immediately start twisting the strings dangling from the cuffs of my pant legs between my fingers. I try to sit still but I can't. My laceless sneaker starts toe-tapping to the rhythm the mop bucket made on its journey into my nightmare. That rhythm is stuck in my head. There's something familiar about it. A déjà vu vibe washes over me. My heart rate quickens.

Faster. Faster. Faster.

The faster my heart pounds, the faster my foot taps that familiar rhythm. And now both feet are going.

"You a drummer?" A gravelly voice digs into my ears.

I freeze. Muscles tighten. My heart is pounding in my head.

Should I answer?

I don't know. What should I say?

Opening my mouth to form a word—another feat of strength. My jaw makes a popping sound as I pry open my mouth.

"I dabble. I'm a dabbler," I croak out from between my knees.

Speaking is hard enough. Lifting my head—that will take much more strength. And after that idiotic answer, I'll just keep my head down.

"Huh. Sounds like more than dabbling to me. You got some sick double bass pedal skills from the sounds of those rhythmic feet."

A compliment? For me? This guy just flipped us into Topsy-Turvy World.

I debate whether or not to pry my head off my knees. This guy speaks my language. But I don't think I'm ready to look him, or anyone, in the face right now. I'll probably see two or three of him, considering the feeling of whatever shit this Hell hole has forced into me.

I hesitate.

Slowly, I start to lift my head. But first, I start with my eyes, and his feet.

Long, narrow feet in standard non-skid black shoes, with scuffed up toes. What's not standard are the black and white music note shoelaces.

Man, oh man, I miss my laces. I can barely keep my Converse on my feet without laces. They keep flopping off and thudding against the floor with every step I take. The noise draws too much attention. I don't like that at all. And tripping. They keep tripping me up. Another attention getter. It sucks. What, they think I can't kill myself or someone else if I don't have shoelaces? Ha! Believe me, if I want to kill someone, that job will get done *with* or *without* laces.

Okay, stop obsessing about shoelaces.

Yep. Sure enough. As my eyes roll up his legs, I see he is tall and skinny. His feet implied that before my eyes confirmed it.

"It's okay. I don't bite," he says as he leans down and squeezes the handle of the mop head until the water stops dripping into the bucket. "And I don't judge."

"Yeah, *that* must be hard working *here*." Wow! That felt effortless. I didn't even think about it. But the croaking. Holy shit do I need a drink of water.

Before I finish that water-thought, the janitor calls out into the hallway. "Nurse, could we get a cup of water in here, please? . . . Thanks." He leans the mop against the padded wall.

After peeling off his blue rubber glove, he reaches out his hand toward me. It's tatted. A psychedelic black and gray skull surrounded in a swirling mist covers the top. Across his knuckles, in black block letters, is the word L-I-V-E. "Tommy. The name's Tommy. And you are?"

It takes me a minute to move my arm. I feel like I need to oil my joints, like the Tin Man, to outstretch my limb. Then, as I reach out to make contact, my hair gets tangled around the button on the cuff of my sleeve. My face heats up. My hair pulls my sleeve up before finally snapping free. By the time hand touches hand, my stitches are showing.

Damn it! Not a good first impression. Oh, wait. I almost forgot where I am.

I still haven't looked him in the face. I just stare at our shaking hands. Blurry at first. Soon veiny highways appear, pulsing and weaving around age-spots and in and out of skull orifices. Then I notice his scar. A red line running up his inner forearm has been worked into another tattoo— the thin red line stands as the veil between worlds.

"You're a lefty?" I look him in the face.

A crooked smile emerges. He has a dimple. No. Wait. That's the tip of another scar, faint, that runs up along his cheekbone. A strand of black, disheveled hair has fallen out of his ponytail and hangs in his eyes. I can't see their color. I don't dare look too closely.

"Ambidextrous," he says as he swipes his hair out of his line of sight.

Brown. His eyes are brown, almost black.

I turn away. Our hands are still clasped together.

Still shaking.

"Huh. Funny. Me too."

Hands stop shaking but remain joined. He laughs. "Yeah, funny."

"You asked for water?" Nurse Hatchet floats in with a small plastic cup half full.

Tommy reaches behind him with his right hand. His eyes remain on me. I can feel them. "Thanks. That'll be all." He takes the cup and hands it to me. "Here. This will kill the frog in your throat."

I let go of his hand. My palm is sweaty.

As I take a sip of water, he says, "Your name. I didn't get your name."

I almost choke when I cough out, "That's because I didn't tell you."

CHAPTER 4

Everyone is calling me by something other than my real name. Well, the few people who talk to me at all, that is. When your eyes stay riveted to the floor, it doesn't welcome a whole lot of conversation from others, not even small talk, which I detest anyway. Small talk is for the small minded.

There's a knock on the door frame of my closet-room. Followed by, "How you doin' today, Dabbler."

I turn around and see Tommy standing there. He has one hand wrapped around a push broom handle, and the other is stuffed in the pocket of his Dickies.

My throat is so dry I don't speak. I nod and raise my free hand. A small nub of a crayon is in my other hand trying to finish a doodle I've been hiding in for hours. It's that time of day when patients can go to the dayroom to socialize, read year-old magazines, watch TV, play board games together, or stare at one another like their ready to slice someone open and scrape their bones.

I draw instead. It's safe. It frees the mind. Most of all, it's a great hiding space.

Tommy leans his head out into the hallway, looking in one

direction and then the other. Then he takes a step into my closet, as he eases his pocketed hand out where I can see. There's something in his grip. I stare, trying to clear my foggy vision enough to see what the small object is.

"I snatched a couple markers from the dayroom for you. Probly work better than that near-death crayon you got there." Holding them out for me, that crooked smile of his emerges, along with his scar-dimple.

The markers are sitting right there on his open palm for me to take—one black and one orange. I want to take them. I really do. But I can't stop staring at his scar. "What happened to your face?" I blurt out. The frog in my throat has leapt out of my control. Yeah, this is why I try to keep to myself. Stupid. Stupid. Stupid me.

I turn away. My left hand automatically starts doodling again. "Sorry. I mean your scar. What happened?"

Tommy takes a step closer and places the markers beside my doodle pad. "Here. Add some orange to that flaming Jack-O-Lantern head. Halloween's right around the corner." He rests the broom handle against the side of the desk, then reaches up and runs his finger back and forth along his scarred cheek. "Oh, and this right here? This should show you that *I* don't think you're delusional."

My doodling hand freezes. I glance up at him over my shoulder.

"Yeah, that's right." His nonchalant-stare-off-into-nowhere look switches to an intense stare, as he turns and looks at me through the two strands of hair dangling in his face.

Those dark chocolate colored eyes look like black holes ready to transport me to other worlds, other dimensions. My twitchy mind is tugging at me, trying to make me turn away. But I can't move. For some uncontrollable reason I can't look away.

"I know about the cutters, the junkies." He touches his scarred cheek again. "First hand."

I quickly try rolling away on the stability ball, my seat. (Yeah, *now* they won't let me have a chair in my room. I could use it as a weapon—again.) I fall backward onto the floor. I guess the ball doesn't work like a chair on wheels. And stability? Ha! Did they *forget* where I *am*? *Who* I am? I can barely sit still in a stationary chair. How the Hell did they think I'd be able to work this stand-in?

Crab-crawling away, my back soon hits the bathroom door-frame. A dead end. No escape. I'm getting cut. He's going to scrape my bones.

Tommy leans down toward me. My breath gets stuck in my throat. He places his hand on the ball, rolls it toward him, and takes a seat. Leaning forward, with his elbows on his knobby knees, he starts telling me his tale. "Where you are now, I once was. This scar? This is not my work." He holds out his left arm, forearm up, and pulls up his sleeve. "This here. *This* is my work. Not the tat. The veil. There's a very thin line between life and death. The land of the living and the land of the dead. I've crossed that line and live to tell about it." He rolls his arm over and makes a fist, displaying the L-I-V-E tattoo on his knuckles. "Don't let those crazy junkie-cutters push you over that line. Not everyone makes it back across."

Still not breathing, shoulders cranked up near my ears, all I can do is nod my head. I don't speak. I don't move a limb.

Tommy opens his fist. He rolls his hand over, palm up and open. Then he nods.

I hesitate. My shoulders drop. Then I grasp his rough hand. A crooked smile emerges on *my* face, as Tommy pulls me up onto my feet.

CHAPTER 5

THAT STUPID, smiley redhead sent me there *again*! How the Hell did she *get* this job? I swear, a prerequisite for getting hired in this shithole—all employees need to have been a mental patient at some point in the past.

There's the circle of junkies, scars wriggling and writhing like serpents with ADHD. This time there are no chairs. Everyone is sitting on a pillow on the floor. And as soon as I step into the room, every face turns and stares at me—the Chair Chucker.

Yeah, that's what this group calls me. Chair Chucker. Glaring eyes pierce my flesh. I'm sure they're imagining how much dust they can scrape from my bones before someone breaks up the insanity.

Next to the door is a pile of throw pillows. Outside of the door, still looking in at me, is Nurse Hatchet. Her Cheshire perma-grin is screaming, "We're all mad here." My sweaty hand slips from the doorknob and I reach down and grab a cushy seat. This seat does not join the circle. It stays near the door. Why my hands are not incessantly scratching my head, I can't figure it out. It must have something to do with whatever meds they've given me. I can't keep track of them all.

Why haven't I continued to pocket them? Some staff are more vigilant than others. I pocket when I can. Knees hugged in to my chest, I'm ready. If I sit crossed legged or on my knees, I could get the tingles.

No way am I letting that happen.

Unable to look into the circle of patients, I hear muffled talking. I don't know what it's all about. The voices sound far away. Trying harder to make out the words, I all of a sudden realize the voices are getting louder, closer. My heart is pounding so hard I feel like a cartoon character whose chest protrudes with every beat. Then I make the mistake of looking up from the floor.

Then the blackout comes.

CHAPTER 6

THE PADDED ROOM should get reassigned as my room. I get escorted in every day. Thrown in is more like it. One of my shoulders feels dislocated from the landings. Why do they always have to drop me on the same side? *Idiots*! Emphasis on the idiot label. They've sent me to the wrong counseling group, the same group of junkie-cutters, every day for my *entire* first week. What is wrong with these people?

I'm not a fucking junkie!

As I'm lying in a puddle of my own sweat from yet another freak-out escape from Junkie-Cuttersville, chest heaving from the struggle, the particulars of my Blue-Papered admittance to this psycho hospital come back to me in movie-preview-like snippets. I wish I could piece it all together, but you know what they say about wishes—be careful.

My roommate outside the psych hospital is a whore, I know, but we're pretty good friends, have been since high school. With a different "boyfriend" every week, I lose track of who is her current partner. It sickens me, but it's not *my* life.

Our friendship is what you would call habitual at this point in our late twenties. It's not easy for me to make friends, so I tend to hold onto whoever will stick around. Jill sticks around. Though, I'm sure after what went down last we saw each other, she may reconsider. I probably no longer have a place to live whenever I'm allowed to return to the outside world, which is filled with even more psychos.

My last night of freedom, I woke in the middle of the night to the sound of Jill screaming. Not so unusual. But it's what she was screaming that made me react the way I did.

"Get off me you sick fuck!" Then I heard a crash followed by, "Stop! No! Stop! Help!"

Some people see red. I see black.

The next thing I remember is Jill pulling me off some buff surfer-looking dude with a spray-on tan, a receding hairline, and buck teeth. Well, he had buck teeth until I knocked them out with one swing of the wooden baseball bat.

That bat, the one we'd always kept beside the door in case of a break-in, yeah, well, it's no longer functional. I busted it in the scuffle. I don't even remember the scuffle after the first swing of the bat. What I do remember…

The whole apartment was smashed up. I was screaming and swinging the remains of a slit-in-two bat, splintered on its stunted end. Apparently, at some point the cops had busted through our front door. One officer had to duck from a swing. (In my defense, I wasn't aware the cops were even there, let alone in the way of my swing.) Surfer-wannabe was spitting out blood and still holding a handful of his own teeth, even though his hands were cuffed behind his back. He could barely see through his swollen eyes. A frazzled Jill was still naked and never, as far as I'm aware, attempted to put on clothes the entire time this all went down. (Yeah, I told you she's a whore. Her Daddy didn't hug her enough as a child. Or maybe he hugged her a bit *too* much.)

What I remember clear as day is when Jill told the cops, "It was a misunderstanding, officers. He wasn't raping me. We were role playing a rape fantasy. Then *she* went off her rocker like some crazy meth-head."

That's all I needed to hear.

"A rape fantasy?! You've obviously never been raped for real —that would turn your sick fantasy into a fucking nightmare, you stupid whore. And you, you surfer-wannabe-rapist…"

I don't remember what else I said. But I do remember somehow breaking free from the cops hold on me.

Then all went back to black.

I woke up right here, in this same padded room, foggy at best, seeing double and triple of whatever staff was attending to me. And my arms, they were focused on my arms, my scars.

It seems like a dream now, but thinking back, I swear, as they were examining my scars someone said, "Looks like we got ourselves another one."

Maybe they just meant another suicidal.

But with their insistence on placing me in a counseling group with those junkie-cutters, they must think I'm one of them.

But they act like they don't know how those particular junkies get their fix. Like I'm delusional when I tell them about the bone dust. And their scars. What does the staff think *those* are about?

Oh, yeah, could be just plain old cutters who happen to be junkies, too.

I look down at my wrists and see the dotted scars running from left to right and right to left. My naïve first suicide attempt with a serrated knife, a weak will, and no clue how to get the job done. Yeah, those could get mistaken for track marks, I *guess*. But on my wrists? Well, there are nice plump veins to tap into in that spot.

I shiver at the thought.

But still… No. That doesn't make any sense. Why would I run and scream for help from my own kind?

Lazy. Just label me with the diagnosis-tag "with psychotic tendencies" and it explains it all away, while masking their unwillingness to actually dig to the bottom of what's really going on with me.

"Get 'em in, drug 'em up to drool-mode, and get' em out. We need the bed for the next patient with insurance." That's the psycho hospital game.

Then out on the streets there's a bunch of doped up zombies walking around talking to themselves and to the invisible person next to them, swinging their arms at who knows what, while passersby move to the other side of the street trying to not catch the psycho virus.

Medicated Zombification.

So, I pocket my meds every chance I get.

Oh yeah, and I still haven't met with a psychiatrist. I've been in here for a week. Do they think I'm going to miraculously figure this all out on my own, while drugged up on who knows what cocktail of psychotropics that they inject me with every time they toss me into the padded cell?

Even if I could figure it all out, no one will believe me. I'm psychotic, remember?

The padded door scrapes open. I don't look to see who is entering. Total exhaustion prevents me from rolling over to face the door. My sleeve slides up my arm. A gloved hand latches on and sticks me with a needle.

More drugs? I can't even move. Why do they need to drug me?

I don't want to play this game anymore. I quit.

Please, just…

CHAPTER 7

I WAKE to the smell of my own stomach bile. An acrid stench. With all this vomiting, I'll certainly have no problem shedding that stubborn ten pounds that's been taunting me. Who needs healthy diet and exercise? Not this psycho.

Skinny jeans, here I come.

Padding scrapes against padding. I roll over. The door is opening slowly. I can't see who's there. All is a blur.

Then I hear a gravelly, "Nurse, a cup of water, please." I rub the drug fog from my eyes.

A hand is gripping the edge of the door. L-I-V-E is peeking in at me.

A minute or so later enters Tommy, with mop handle in one hand and a cup of water in the other.

Shaking his shaggy head, he hands me the water. "We really need to stop meeting like this, Dabbler."

I'm barely able to smile, but I try. With the numb feeling that fills me, it probably looks more like constipation than relief to see an understanding face.

A muffled conversation is going on outside the door. Tommy takes a couple steps into my cell. When I rise up onto my elbow, the one that isn't attached to the arm with what feels like a dislocated shoulder, I see a shaggy- multilayered-mullet-headed psychiatric technician sitting guard beside the open door. His black Chinos are so tight they're forcing a fat roll above and below the belted waist. The way his chair is angled, I can see his facial expression as he's obviously flirting with Nurse Hatchet. His wide, mesmerized eyes and hungry grin. Her giggles, and the way she brushes her long red hair behind her ear.

Get a room already. Blast some Whitesnake. You know you want to.

Tommy glances over his shoulder toward the guard dog. "I'm surprised they allowed a chair so close to you." He nudges my laceless Converse with the toe of his work shoe.

The sneaker falls right off my foot as we both snigger.

He eases the door a bit closer to closed, just enough so that the flirty couple can't see inside. Then he crouches down beside me. "You're not a user at all, are you?"

I shake my head. Everything spins.

Tommy hands me the cup of water. I reach for it but miss, grasp air. He places it in my hand. I take a sip and clear my throat. "I experimented in my late teens, early twenties. Wasn't for me. I like to have control of my mind." Turning away, I laugh at the idea that I have *any* control over my mind, even without abusing drugs. "But never the needle. Opiates . . ." I shake my head in disgust and look back at Tommy. "Not my thing." I feel the question in his stare. "They hit too close to home, and let's just say...home is *not* where *my* heart is."

Rolling up his sleeve, the one on the arm with the thin red line and tat, he leans a little closer to me. "See the shooting stars right there on the left side?" He points to the specs of light in the tail of the star near the crook of his elbow.

I squint and look closer to figure out what he's trying to show me. I pull myself away when I realize, "Track marks?"

He unfurls his sleeve and straightens his back. "Seven years clean today. Heroin may have stolen years from my life, but I don't regret one minute of it." He rubs his chin and glances up, as though looking to the heavens. "Well, maybe a few minutes of regret here and there." He laughs and looks back at me. "No. But really. It made me who I am today. Which is—a Hell of a lot smarter that I was back then. And..." He glances over his shoulder toward the slightly ajar door, "It clued me in to the *real* monsters in the junkie world. It's not the poor hacks wielding the heroin-filled needle. It's not the pill poppers stealing Grandma's pain meds. It's those crazy cutters, ready to slice open their next victim to save themselves a whole lot of pain and a little bit of money. Shit." He shakes his head. "Heroin is cheap. Why they have to go it the way they do, we may *never* know."

"That bone dust must bring on one *Hell* of a high." My throat is so scratchy I drink the rest of my water in one gulp.

"Who knows? Maybe it comes with one super immense orgasm to boot."

Water shoots out of my mouth and showers the padded wall, followed by laughter I haven't heard come from my mouth in months.

"Well, if that's the case then sign me up." I almost laugh again, but it gets stuck in my throat and comes out as a heavy sigh instead. "Yeah, ah…no. I can't make *that* into a joke, it's too horrific. What the fuck is wrong with people? I just don't get it."

"Us rational minded folks can't even begin to understand the irrational. Their minds aren't wired the same as ours."

A smile emerges on my face so big it hurts my cheeks.

Tommy's brow furrows, as he cocks his head and squints at me with curiosity.

"You called me 'rational minded.'" I glance away, but I can't stop smiling.

He chuckles. "That's because you are. What's a few suicidal

thoughts and a little anxiety? Shit. Everyone's guilty of one or the other, if not both, at some point in their lives. Someone tries to tell me they ain't never, and I'll show you a liar." He starts to mop up my vomit. Then he speaks out of the corner of his mouth when he asks, "You're pocketing your meds every chance you get, right?"

I shush him as I motion toward the door with my thumb. Then I nod.

"That's the work of a rational mind, my sista," he whispers as he leans down and nudges my shoulder with his elbow.

Sista? Huh. I don't really consider that a term of endearment.

My only sibling robbed me blind, slashed my tires, and turned me in for growing marijuana.

That idiot pill-junkie-dealer—she had no idea I was legal, growing medicinal. Who needs enemies with family like that?

All of a sudden Tommy's waving his free hand back and forth in front of my face. "Hell-o? You in there? Where'd that smile go?"

I shake my head free of the intrusive memories. Raising my cup to my mouth, I unclench my jaw to take a sip, but the water's gone. I throw the cup at the wall. It hits the floor just a couple feet in front of me.

"Tip: If you wanna release some tension, don't throw an empty plastic cup."

I glance up at Tommy. A tight-lipped smirk eases across my face. "Yeah. Throw a chair instead. Much more satisfying."

Neither one of us can hold back the laughs.

The padded door eases open a little wider. "Hey! She's not in there for social hour, Tommy," the David Coverdale wannabe shouts over his shoulder from his guard post. "Just mop and go."

"Hey, Douche! News flash: This *isn't* the 1980's, you're *not*

David Coverdale, and that *isn't* Tawny Kitaen. Get a clue." Tommy's hand is squeezing his mouth shut, as he's trying not to burst out laughing. Then I finish with, "Oh, and pulling your belt tighter *doesn't* make you look any *less fat*."

Now *I'm* covering *my* mouth. Where did that come from? I don't even feel like I just said that. It's like I had some freak out-of-body experience or something.

As Tommy's trying to mop, he keeps tucking his face into his shoulder to muffle his laughter. It's not working very well.

Through the wider opening of the door I see the Nurse. She's still smiling, even after my insult. She hugs her clipboard to her chest, pulls her hair forward over her shoulder—a wave of flames—and skulks away.

Brushing aside the laughter with a shake of his head, Tommy turns toward me with a serious expression. His tone matches as he says, "All joking aside. I hope I didn't say something to make you angry. That wasn't my intention, I hope you know."

"No. No worries. I know. It's just..." I turn away. "It's what you called me. 'Sista' isn't what I consider a flattering term... Family... Ha! What a joke."

He crouches down and rests his hand on my shoulder. "I *feel* that. Believe me. I know; blood doesn't equal family. Brothers." He pokes his thumb at his chest. "You learn through experience —choose your family wisely. If you let blood dictate who your family is, you could likely end up bled to death."

I laugh a tight-chested titter, as I glance down at my scarred forearms. "Yeah, you can say that again."

CHAPTER 8

I HEAR whispers in the shadows. Wide awake and facing the wall, I pretend I'm sleeping.

"Ssh. Git out of my ass, Toodles. Let sleeping dogs lay."

"Lie."

"What? I'm not lying, you idiot. Don't wake her before we slice and dust. We need to git this done and then git out. You git me *now*?"

"Yeah. Yeah. Got the knife. Here."

My heart revs up and starts pounding in my head. Frozen, I listen for footsteps. As soon as it sounds like they're right beside me, I flip around and hold my pillow up in front of me for protection. Hell, it's all I've got. A popping and tearing sounds out. I scream as feathers start spilling from my pillow. I scramble back against the wall and feathers fly everywhere. I can't see my attackers through the feathery veil, but I hear scuffling feet and stumbling bodies tripping toward the door. Then I hear a metallic clattering. The legs of the psych tech's chair against the linoleum floor.

My twenty-four hour watch has woken? Let's hope, so he can catch those monsters.

What's left of my pillow gets tossed to the floor. The whisperers have vanished. No one is at my door. Scurrying footsteps race down the hallway.

I ease out of bed, careful not to make a sound. I see something shimmering under the desk in the ray of light shining in from the hallway. Unsure what it is, I reach down to pick it up. Thinking twice, I halt before making contact. I lean in for a closer look.

A silver-colored toothbrush.

But not your standard toothbrush. This one is shaved around the edges and at the tip.

A shank?!

I *am* in a fucking prison after all. Should I pick it up, take it with me? Or leave it and show the staff?

They'll probably blame me for planting it to try to convince them I'm not delusional. But the guard dog—he can back up my story, right?

I leave the shank and peek out the door. No one is in sight. No one is responding. Where the Hell is the guard dog? Why isn't anyone concerned about screams in the middle of the night?

Oh yeah, I remind myself, psycho hospital.

A short distance down the hall to the right of my room, at the T-intersection of the corridors, I see the tall staff desk counter, but I see no staff. No one at all. To the left of my room I see the psych tech's chair is now two bedrooms away from mine, flipped on its side in the middle of the hall. A trace trail of feathers still flutters about.

Fingers crossed that the psych tech is in pursuit of my attackers.

Then I hear and see a door quietly click shut. The last bedroom on the left.

For a moment, all is silent. But as I strain to listen for, well, anything, I think I hear music coming from the right. Barely audible from where I'm standing, but it's definitely music coming from somewhere.

A subtle soundtrack to my nightmare.

Lovely. Someone is enjoying tunes while I'm almost carved open and dusted.

I sneak quietly into the hall and take a couple steps to the T-intersection of the corridors. I peer around the corner. My heart revs up even faster.

My twenty-four hour watch. He's leaning on the shelf of the half-door of the nurse's station—Med Central—flirting with Tawny Kitaen. They're laughing, with the sound of classic rock emanating from behind Nurse Hatchet. The Stones—"Sympathy for the Devil."

Lovely. I have no witness. I'm fucked.

Someone's head pops up out of paperwork-mode and is now visible behind the tall staff's counter. Another psych. tech. A long blonde braid hangs over the shoulder of a middle-aged woman I've never seen before. She shoots an angry glare toward the nurse's station. "Am I the only one who just heard that?"

No response.

So, I guess everyone around here waits for someone *else* to respond to a crisis.

Before she turns toward my direction, I hit the floor and slither my way over to the front of the counter and slide to the end corner to spy what's up. I want to know where the fuck everyone is. Why isn't anyone doing their job? I know it's shitty third shift work in a psycho hospital, but at least it's a job—do it to the best of your ability, for fuck sake! Lives depend on it.

I hear the braided woman stand up so fast her chair tips backward and tumbles against the floor. "I guess I have to do everything around here." Then she mumbles, "What the fuck is new?" as I hear her clink open the lock of a file cabinet drawer, pull it out, and shuffle around the confidential paperwork inside.

Oh yes. Make sure you finish your paperwork before you respond to a potential crisis.

Still crouched down, I wait until I hear that all three staff members are at the nurse's station. They're in a quiet confrontation about job responsibilities.

What a joke!

But now's my chance.

I slip-slide my stocking feet as fast and as soundlessly as I can back to my room. I grab the shank from under the desk and slip it into my shirt. Placing the makeshift blade under my boobs, I make sure to wrap the thick elastic material of my bra around it for safekeeping. I grab my Converse and bolt.

CHAPTER 9

"Who are you?"

"Well, hello and good evening to you."

She can't be any older than maybe nineteen or twenty, with her seamless caramel skin and wide wondering eyes. And she's in the janitor's closet? Not what I expected to find.

"No time for pleasantries," I say as sweat drips from my temples. "I need help. Where's Tommy?"

"He's off tonight." Her dark chocolate colored eyes stare at me as she slowly raises a hand and points at my head. "Uh, you *might* want to stop scratching." She reaches her other hand behind her, pulls a white cloth out of the belt of her Dickies, and then hands it to me. "Don't worry, it's clean."

I freeze, then pull my hand away from my wet head and reach for the towel to wipe away the sweat. But when I grab the white cloth I see red.

Blood. All over my hand and now all over the towel.

Swiping the cloth over my temple and across my hairline causes a stinging sensation. Gritting my teeth, I wince and my eyes start filling with pools of pain.

I had no idea I'd been scratching.

"Maybe you should see a nurse about that."

"Hell no! I can't go to them. They already think I'm crazy. They'll never believe what just happened." I start scratching again, but flinch and quickly stop when I feel the raw and tender bald spot on my head. What little peach fuzz that had started growing back is now gone. "You must have something to help me out. Anything. *Please.*"

"I don't have any bandages or Neosporin." She shrugs as she glances around the janitor's walk-in closet. "Sorry. I wish I *could* help. I *really* do."

Raising up the blood soaked cloth in my hand, I look around at the surrounding wall-to-ceiling metal shelving: spray bottles, buckets of bleach, jugs of various cleaning solutions, boxes and boxes of plastic gloves...aha—piles of cleaning cloths.

As I reach to grab a couple towels, I knock over a stack of them onto the floor. "Sorry. I didn't mean to make a mess," I say as I crouch to pick it all up.

The young girl quickly reaches out one of her hands, which is now gloved, to block my efforts. "No. Stop. It's all right. Really. Let *me* clean that up."

I look at my bloody hand that's about to grab a bunch of clean white cloths from the floor. Shaking my head, I pull away. "Sorry. Really, truly, I'm *so* sorry." I lean my back against one of the tall shelves, drop on my ass, and bury my stinging head in my blood stained hands. And the tears are now flowing like blood-filled rivers.

Stupid, stupid me. Now this girl will *never* help me, even if she could. To her I'm just another psycho.

Something bumps my knee. I glance up. "Here. Take these. They didn't touch the floor."

Through blurry vision I see she's handing me a couple of the cloths. The sympathetic expression on her face makes me think of Tommy. I wish he was here right now. He'd know what to do. He'd *believe* me.

I try smiling, though it's tough and probably looks fake. "Thank you." I take the towels and start tying one of them around my head like a bandana. "When's Tommy's shift? He knows what's what around here. Uh—No offense."

A timid expression takes over her face, as she glances away and tucks a couple of her dreads behind her ear. "No. None taken. Dad's better in a crisis than me. He's been here many years. I'm just working my way through college." She hands me a third towel. "He should be here around seven."

It takes a few seconds for her words to sink in. I wipe my eyes and look into hers. Dark chocolate. Familiar. Then, when I reach to take the towel from her, it hits me.

My hand freezes in mid-reach. "Dad?"

"Yeah. He got me the job here. He said the overnight shift… it's less crazy." She lets a tense laugh slip out.

My hand drops to my bouncing knee as I sigh. "Nights? In a psycho hospital? Less crazy?" I shake my head. "Sounds like he's never worked the nightshift before."

"No. He said there are less Incident Reports from nights than from days."

Now I laugh. "Gee, I wonder why that is. Huh."

She leans down and reaches toward my forehead with the towel. My heart skips as I think to pull away. But I don't. I allow her to wipe blood from my face. She smells like sandalwood and lavender. I breathe her in.

"I have to go clean all the meeting rooms before my shift ends, but you can stay in here. Hide. Whatever." She tosses the bloody towel in a hazardous materials receptacle. "I'll play dumb if someone finds you."

When she stands back up, I stand with her and reach out my

hand. "The name's Dory. But just call me Dabbler; your Dad does."

Our hands meet. We shake.

"Sunshine, that's what he calls me. But around here I'm known as Irie."

"Huh. I hope that's a message for me from the cosmos."

"It is what you want it to be." She turns and grabs the mop handle and wheels the bucket it's in toward the door. Before she exits, she looks over her shoulder at me. "It's nice to meet a fellow Marley fan." She flashes the peace sign. "One love."

How does she know? Then I realize the Marley tank I'm wearing under my button-down shirt.

CHAPTER 10

A CRINKLING SOUND right next to my ear wakes me. My neck is so cramped I can barely lift my head off my knees. Why am I in this position, *and* on the floor?

"Wakey, wakey, time to find an escapey." Someone nudges my Converse.

When I can finally lift my head all the way up and open my eyes, I see Tommy standing in front of the closed janitor's room door. Something silver and shiny is wrapped around my shoulders. The crinkling. I throw it off me with a shrug of my shoulders.

"Sunshine—she's a good egg. Used the emergency blanket I gave her to make sure you stayed warm." He shakes his head in disbelief. "I don't know how *my* kid turned out so great, but, man, am I grateful. Ha! Grateful she takes after her mother."

"Who are you kidding? You would have done the same thing. Don't sell yourself short."

"Yeah, well, I wasn't always like this. It's a wonder Irie didn't end up another junkie, a drunk deadbeat, or dead—murdered, like her mother."

Now I shake *my* head in disbelief. "Murdered? Well, now I'm wide awake. What the Hell happened?" Rolling my head side to side to crack out the kinks, I realize how inconsiderate that sounded. "Sorry. I didn't mean to sound insensitive. Sorry for your loss."

"No worries." He looks down, feet fidgeting and twisting about. Then he leans down to tie is already tied work shoe. "That was seven long years ago. We've healed. Well, I've healed." His music-notes-shoelace is now neatly double tied, bows evenly looped and hanging on either side of the black leather, nonskid shoe. Then he glances up at me. "Here." He grabs a couple clean white cloths off the shelf next to him and tosses them to me. "You *really* look insane with those bloody rags tied around your head. Might want to clean yourself up." With the raising of his chin, he motions toward the sink in the back corner of the closet-room. I hadn't even noticed it last night; it's hidden beside the monstrous shelving.

"Can't fool me. I know that tactic. Have used it all my life. Now spill." I stand and step over to the sink.

"Tactic?"

"Yeah. The old change the subject and turn the attention to the other person to avoid talking about an uncomfortable subject." As I turn on the water faucet, I look over my shoulder to see his response.

Chin down, he glances up and, with an amused smile, looks at me through the strands of hair that have fallen out of his ponytail and are dangling on either side of his face. And there's that scar-dimple.

"Are *you* the counselor now?"

"Hey, I've been in counseling for most of my life; I know the role well. And..." I playfully splash water at him with the flick of my hand. "You're *doing* it again."

"Let's just say, Kaya—that's my wife's name...*was* my wife's name..." He rubs his forehead with his gloved hand. "Boy, I hate saying that. Anyway, she was a black woman. Look at me." He raises his arms out to each side. "A living breathing stereotype—Native American drunk and junkie. Then look at Irie. And, as you already know, this damned world is full of intolerant people. That should tell it all." He reaches up and touches his scarred cheek. "Well, and that's when *this* happened. They were intolerant Dusters, or, as you like to call them—junkie-cutters. Dusted Kaya before killing her, just to torture us all, and then the crazy fuckers tried to dust me. Ha! *That* didn't turn out the way they'd planned." All of a sudden he halts the prepping for his shift he's been doing while he talks, and he looks sidelong at me. "Hey, wait a minute." He points at me. "You're good."

I turn and face him. "Why, whatever are you talking about?" I play dumb.

"You're the one with the bloody head who hid in the janitor's closet and slept here on the floor to escape something unbearable. The subject should be on *you*, Deflector."

"What? No. I'm Dabbler. Remember?"

"Yeah, dabbling in some crafty avoidance tactics. What the Hell went on here last night? Sunshine told me you were freaked the fuck out, shaking and shit, and didn't even realize you were scratching yourself to death. It scared her. Brought back horrible visions of her mother's murder."

"Wait. What? She saw it happen?"

"I don't want to talk about it." He looks away, hesitates a moment, then looks right back at me and laughs. "Hey, you're doing it again. Stop that. It's time for *you* to spill. Let's have it —*all* of it. Go." He points at me and waits.

Taking in a deep breath, I pivot and plant my ass on the

bench beside the sink. My breath releases and it all starts to come back to me. I reach into my shirt and pull the shank out of my bra. "We need to *stop* those junkie-cutter-psycho-Duster-fucks before they attack or 'dust' someone else."

Wide-eyed and mouth open, Tommy leans on the shelf and takes in my tale.

CHAPTER 11

FEET ON THE DOOR FRAME, midsection twisting and turning and trying to break free, I'm practically growling at the three male psych. techs. holding my upper body and trying to force me into the junkie-cutters counseling group again.

Nurse Hatchet is watching, smiling.

"Stop! Let. Me. Go. Argh… I'm not a junkie. This is NOT my group."

By this time in the struggle, the sleeves of my shirt are cranked up my arms, scars out in the open for all to see. Oh, yeah, and one of the psych techs is cupping a boob again. Good thing I moved the shank to my sock instead of my bra.

"Yeah. Yeah. That's what they all say. Those scars tell the real story. Now stop struggling. You know you're going in there one way or another." David Coverdale, with his forced fat roll jiggling against my back and his strawberry-scented mullet swaying this way and that, thinks he's got power over me.

"These are not junkie-cuts on my arms. I wanted to die, not scrape my fucking bones, you sick fucks!"

"Bone-scraping talk again," Coverdale says. "I *told* you she's delusional."

I turn to the perv with sandpaper hands and doughnut dust around his lips. "Stop touching my tits, you fucking pervert!"

My breasts are immediately freed from The Boob's sandpaper cup. (Yes, his name is now The Boob. His real name doesn't matter. Not to me.) He readjusts his hands. The save-his-job-move weakens his hold on me. Moving my feet higher up on either side of the doorframe, I allow slack in my knees. But only for a split second. It's time to put my runner's legs to work.

With my legs at a forty-five degree angle bend, I push off the frame with all the strength and anger I have. The three psych. techs. are shoved back across the hall and fall on their asses, with me on top of the dung pile, like a fly ready to take flight. And I do.

In this jumbled mess, it's easy to slip my arm free from the one guy who still tries to keep a hold of me. His grip has weakened significantly with the fall. When I scramble to get away and get a solid footing, I see that the Dusters have front row seats at the door to watch the chaos.

They look like they're jonesing for a fix. I scramble faster and dash away down the long hall, without a clue where I'm headed. Freak outs tend to scramble my thinking.

Then I remember my talk with Tommy—our plan. As I'm scurrying down the hall, passed my open bedroom door, I glance over my shoulder and see that the psych. techs. haven't yet made it around the corner of the T-section in the corridor. I take a chance and run straight to the end of the hall and into... the last bedroom on the left.

CHAPTER 12

THE BEDSPRINGS SQUEAK above my head and the frame hits the wall, pinching my shoulder between them, as the heavyset Duster plops onto the mattress. I'm not sure if it's Toodles—whoever the Hell that is—or the one with the terrible grammar—Git Girl. But I know damn well this is the room those two psychos ran into after attacking me the other night. With shank in hand, I'm ready just in case they find me before I hear the knock on the door—my cue.

But the door hasn't yet closed. I hear sniffling.

That dirty Duster better not infect me with her Cutter's Flu.

The sniffles cease at the same instance I hear feet shuffling into the room. Then the door clicks shut.

The bedsprings squeak again and the frame shimmies a bit, as the Duster on top moves about above my head. My shoulder is freed from the pinch against the wall. Now I can move my head enough to see the new arrival's feet—dirty white Keds on the ends of gray stick legs.

"You can roll over and hide your face, but you're not fooling me."

"Just git. Leave me alone!"

"How long's it been?"

"Just. Git. Now!"

"Listen. I know I'm just a newbie, but I need to know. If not for your sake, then for mine. How long before it happens to me?"

"There you go, thinking of yourself." An earthquake shakes the bed as Git Girl moves about. Finally, after what sounds like a bit of a struggle moving the mass of her body, she gets up out of bed.

I see her size ten green Crocs hit the floor and then shuffle fast across the small room toward the door. The dirty white Keds attached to the skinny chicken legs in gray leggings, they get lifted right off the ground as Git Girl slams her up onto the desk beside the door.

Inching my way over a little to get a better look at what's going down, a bed spring that's protruding from the mattress tears my shirt sleeve and gouges my upper arm. I wince and bite back a yelp of pain. From where I'm lying now, I see who I assume is Toodles flat on her back on the top of the desk, kicking her Keds against Git Girl's wide, monstrous thighs as she's on top of Toodles holding her down. She has the neck of Toodles's faded black t-shirt bunched up in her fists, and is almost nose to nose with her. Git Girl growls like a rabid dog. Spittle flies out of her mouth as she's ranting.

"You fool! You never shoulda started. Ha! Such a follower. Now you have *my* pain to look forward to down the road. You like that, *don't* you?" She pulls up on Toodles's t-shirt, squeezing it tight around her neck. Git Girl's fists are forcing Toodles's chin up, cranking her neck at what looks like a very uncomfortable position. "Just something else you can have in common with me, with *someone*, with *anyone*. Commonalities don't equal friendship, especially when they're forced, made-up." She leans in close, sniffs, and then runs her tongue up

Toodles's neck. With her mouth now right next to her ear, she growls, "I should dust you to *death* right now. Better than what's coming for you. What's coming for us all."

"Well, not to death, but, yes, you can get a fix from me. Always. You know that." Toodles is smiling, but I swear I think I see her cheek twitching, trying to hold that pose.

Git Girl releases her grip on Toodles's t-shirt. With one hand flat on her chest holding her down, she reaches around and down with her other hand and slides open the top drawer of the desk. She reaches in and pulls out another shank. Her hand flies up, and she presses the makeshift blade against Toodles's collar bone. Before slicing her open, she leans down and sniffs her again. "You may not be fresh, but *any* dust will do me good… for a *little* while."

Knock-knock-knock, Kno-knock sounds against the door. My cue.

Tommy tries to fling open the door, but it makes a dull *thud* as it slams into Git Girl's big, wide ass. The shank is immediately hustled back into the drawer and the drawer slams shut. Git Girl lies flat against Toodles, and glances at Tommy over her shoulder.

I see L-I-V-E on the edge of the door, holding it open, as I hear him say, "Oh, sorry. I thought you two were still at dinner. I'm here to clean." He tries to poke his head in through the slight opening. He catches a glimpse of me, and I wave him away, trying to mouth him a message.

Our plan to set them up isn't going to work now.

"Oh, who are you trying to kid?" says Git Girl as she turns toward Toodles, leans down, and licks her neck again. She turns back toward Tommy. "You just wanted to catch some girl-on-girl action. We know. Come on in. Wanna join?" She reaches an arm behind her and pats her own fat ass. "Slap it. You know you want to."

Tommy immediately pulls his head out of the room. "No. Really. I'm here to clean. Ah… I'd love to leave you two alone, but I really *do* need to at least clean out the trash." He clears his throat. "Sorry. I *need* to come in."

Git Girl hauls Toodles off the desk by her arm, and plants a noisy wet kiss on her quivering lips. Then the two stroll out of the room arm in arm, Git Girl force-flirting with Tommy over her shoulder as they slither past him into the hallway.

Tommy, half in the room and half in the hall, keeps his eyes toward them, as he ushers me out of hiding with the wave of his hand.

After wiggling my way out from under the bed, I adjust my bunched up jeans and shirt as I shake off the heebie-jeebies. "Gross! They dust each other, too," I whisper. "At least that skinny lackey. She's like a Renfield to that fat psycho bitch." I lean down to put the shank back in my sock. That's when I feel my injured arm.

Right as I'm about to grab hold of the wound to put pressure on it, Tommy hands me a white towel from his cleaning cart that's still in the hallway. "Tie this around it. Tight." He glances out in the hall, looks both ways, even though we're in the last bedroom in this hallway. There's a locked door that punctuates the end. I have no idea where it leads. I've never seen anyone go through it. There is a small square window, filled with check-ered mesh wiring, two-thirds of the way up. It's too high up for me to glance through, but Tommy steps over to it and takes a look. "All's clear. We can talk." He turns back toward me. "What the Hell happened? The plan wasn't to shank yourself." He sees me struggling to tie the cloth around my own arm, and he steps toward me and ties it for me.

"Ha, ha, very funny. It was the damn mattress springs." I look under the tourniquet he just created. "Lovely. Another scar to add to my collection."

"Hey, it just adds more character. Builds mystery." Tommy leans down and grabs the plastic waste bucket from under the desk, then turns and dumps it in the open trash bag hanging from his cart. Before putting the bucket back on the floor, he shrugs and says, "Gotta keep up appearances, make it look legit." He sets the bucket down then stands up and leans against the desk. "Now, what the fuck? Did you have to hear those two going at it?" His shoulders rise to his ears as he makes a grossed out expression—lips curled back and teeth clenched together. Then, all of a sudden, he gasps and cups his mouth with his hand. His eyes grow wider and he pulls his hand away from his mouth. "Ew. Is that how your arm got cut? They were on the bed?"

"No. No. *No.* Stop. Get your mind out of the gutter. They're not lesbians. That was a cover up. Git Girl—the fat one—was about to dust Renfield, I mean Toodles." I shake my head. "I think I like Renfield better. What the Hell is up with a name like Toodles?" Then I remember what they'd said. "She wanted to 'dust her to death,' but, from what I heard, it sounds like Git Girl needs a fix to stop something bad from happening to her, something that won't happen to Toodles, well, not until she's been a user for longer. I guess. I don't know. I don't understand, but this is what I heard." I repeat their conversation to Tommy, as best as I can remember. While I'm talking, Tommy pulls my scratching hand away from my head at least three times.

When my story is over, my head and hands are bloody, a towel is now wrapped around my bloody head as well as my bloody arm, and Tommy's eyes are open wider than I've ever seen anyone's eyes get.

"Well, it doesn't sound like typical withdrawals that this Git Girl is talking about alleviating. Those happen no matter how long you've been using. And the sniffles—you say it sounded like she was crying?"

"That's my only explanation for why she immediately stopped when Toodles walked in."

Tommy nods. "Yeah, don't show your weakness, especially to your lackey. Hmm… Sounds like this bone dust isn't exactly like heroin after all. Maybe withdrawals *do* take longer to kick in, only affecting the long-time users? I don't know. That's my best guess. Plus, who the fuck cares? They deserve to suffer! After what they did to my Kaya, they deserve a Hell of a lot worse than withdrawal pain." By this time in the conversation, Tommy is wringing and twisting a towel in his hands so tight he can't twist it anymore.

"Tommy," I hear someone say from out in the hall, "Who are you talking to?"

We both freeze for a moment, taking in the voice. Then Tommy flips the twisted towel over his shoulder and steps out into the hall. I scurry under the desk and hide. But the chair is at the end of the bed where I can't use it for more cover. I press myself as far back against the wall as I can.

"Ha! Thinking out loud. Bad habit. You caught me." I hear the wheels of Tommy's cleaning cart squeak and get closer to the open doorway.

David Coverdale's voice is louder now. (I can't remember his real name, and I don't care.) It sounds like he's right outside the door with Tommy. "Have you seen Dory? She wasn't in her room when we rounded everyone up for dinner, and I still can't find her. Not a good thing, you know?"

"Dory? Sorry. I don't know who that is. I try not to get to know any of the patients, *especially* not by name. It's a job hazard, if you know what I mean."

"Oh, yeah. I get it. And losing a patient is a big fat dick of a job hazard for me." Coverdale's key-bracelet jingles. I imagine he's taming his wild shag mullet. "Itch-A-Bald Crane, the chick with the bald spot. I think I heard you call her Dabbler. Have you seen her?" "Oh yeah. I remember her. Nope. Sorry. Haven't seen her. Did you try the day room? Maybe she fell asleep in front of the idiot box or got lost in a doodle or something." I hear crinkling trash bags and plastic spray bottles knocking against each other and then a thud on top of the desk. "I've got to get back to work." A spray bottle spritzes something that smells like Lysol. It showers over the front edge of the desk. The desk starts shimmying as Tommy wipes the cleaner around. "Good luck, Rick."

"Let me know if you see her?"

"Yes. I'll do that."

The jingling of the bracelet keys rings out softer and softer as they move away down the hall, accompanied by the scuffing of Rick's heels against the linoleum floor. He's such a slacker he can't even pick his feet up all the way when he walks. I poke my head out from under the desk and look up at Tommy, who's still washing the dry desk top as he stares over his shoulder toward the open doorway.

"Ha! Figures his name is Rick. Now I'll just call him *Dick*." I mumble under my breath, "Huh, call me Itch-A-Bald Crane. Fuck you, Mullet-Master, *Dick*." The towel around my head gets snagged on the wood on the underside of the desk drawer. I pull it all the way off from my head, unsnag it from the desk, and inspect the stains left behind on the cloth. "Hmm . . . not a lethal amount of blood. I think I'll live."

Tommy leans out the doorway and looks down the hall. He turns back and looks down toward me and says, "It's safe to come out. He's gone." He looks back at the desk and continues wiping.

I scoot out of hiding and stand up. While I'm tying the towel around my head again, I see Tommy is zoned out and still wiping the desk. I reach out and put my hand on his to stop him. "If you keep wiping, the desk is going to need a new coat of varnish."

An uncertain laugh escapes him as he shakes his head. A strand of dark hair falls out of his ponytail and dangles down the side of his ruddy face. "Holy. That was close. I thought you were busted." He reaches out and touches my arm, the one with the tourniquet. "Well, this wound looks bad. May need stitches, by the looks of that cloth." He leans out and around the doorframe of the room, and then comes back in and tosses me a clean towel. "Here. Might wanna change that. It's saturated."

Untying the bloody cloth from my wound, I don't look at the cut as I say, "No worries. No need for stitches. I'll just tie this next one," I wave the fresh white cloth like a peace flag, "a lot tighter." As hard as I try, I can't tie it on my own. I shoot Tommy a pleading expression.

"Oh, yeah. Sorry." He steps toward me. "Here. Let me do that." He grabs the towel from my fumbling hand and gently tugs the other end out of my clenched teeth.

While he's tying up my clean tourniquet, I remember the jumble of thoughts that ran through my head while hiding. "Weakness. That's how to get them. Use their weakness against them."

"What are you talking about? We don't know their weakness. How do you suppose we use what we don't know against them?"

I lean on the desk, with my good arm, and drum my fingers on the shiny polished surface. "Hey, I'm already a bloody mess from our first fumble. Feel free to jump in any time with an idea for our next move."

CHAPTER 13

WHY THE HELL did I let Tommy talk me into this? I don't know if I can handle this one.

The doorknob feels like a big round ice cube in my palm. Turning it takes all the strength of character I can dig up from deep inside myself. Before I enter the room, I readjust the bandage under my shirtsleeve, making sure it's not evident I'm injured, have open flesh. But why bother? They will probably smell it on me. Plus, there's only so much I can do to cover up the scabs on my head. The bandana I borrowed from Tommy is thin. If anyone looks close enough, they will be able to see the bumps left behind from my incessant scratching, all that scabbing and re-scabbing.

Good thing I brought the shank. Tommy doesn't know about that. But I refuse to go in alone, unprotected. I'm thankful for long, flare-bottomed jeans right now.

I attempt entering as quietly as possible. But when I ease open the door, all three door hinges cry and scream out, announcing my arrival. Every head in the circle of Dusters turns to see...

"It's the Chair Chucker! Come on in, love. *All* are welcome here."

This surprisingly friendly voice comes from someone that I hadn't heard speak in any of the other group sessions I'd been in. Not that I've actually made it *through* any meetings since the first.

When I look in the direction of the voice, the man's dimpled chin and squinty eyes reveal themselves to me. I'm unsure how to judge him by his appearance, but his fake British accent adds the finishing strokes to his painting of apparent douchery. "Oh, and no offense with the nickname. I find your vigor bloody refreshing." He grabs a pillow from the pile behind him and tosses it in my direction. "Come. Have a seat." He pats the cold, hard linoleum floor on the right just beside him. "Join us." Finger-combing his long bangs out of his face, he smiles a snaggletooth grin.

The dense paisley-print pillow hits me with a dull thud dead in the gut. Unable and unwilling to take my eyes off the group, I fumble with the catch. My seat hits the floor at my feet and my ass soon follows. No way in Hell am I sitting next to him! He's on the other side of the circle, farthest away from the door. I need an unobstructed path as close to my escape route as possible. Then Tommy's words come back to me.

"Make them think you're not afraid; you're one of them. That's the only pathway to their vulnerability."

Taking a deep breath, I stand and pick up my pillow. Brushing all fears out of my way, I head toward the Fake Brit. Nervous laughter comes out of me as I say, "Don't mind me. Old habits and all." Clutching the pillow to my pounding chest, my hand involuntarily cups the wound on my upper arm. Once I realize what I'm doing, I immediately move my hand down to my elbow and hug the pillow tighter.

Snake Girl and Slug Man lean away from one another to form a v-entrance into the circle for me to pass through. Walking away from the door, my only escape, feels like I'm pulling apart two very large magnets. My stride across the open expanse of the empty O feels stuttered, choppy, like the force of the door is holding me back, tugging at me, signaling for me to flee while I still have my life.

When I finally make it across the circle and in front of the wannabe-Brit, I'm repelled by the stench of body odor wafting off from him. I pray he doesn't notice the wincing look that I assume appears on my face the instant his smell invades my nostrils. Remembering my goal, I smile and place my pillow next to him and sit down. Then I realize I can't see a visible scar on him. But he *is* somewhat of a pretty boy—with his high cheekbones, floppy-flirty hair, and that chiseled physique playfully hidden under his somewhat snug button down shirt—so he probably has it hidden somewhere. But that smell! It's so bad I can't look directly at him for very long or I might pass out.

Fake Brit reaches over and pats me on the knee. "I'm chuffed to see you *finally* settle in."

I can't respond. I try but I can't. My words stick in my throat, as I see the cuff of his shirt sleeve ride up his arm just enough to show me the end of a thick and grotesque scar. It starts at his wrist bone, and it appears to run up his outer forearm. He keeps his hand on my knee for an uncomfortably long time. Everything and everyone around us seems awkwardly silent, and time feels like it's slowing down. I can't take my eyes off the scar. Then it starts to move, pulse almost, like something is breathing and wiggling just under the skin, trying to get out. I squeeze my eyes shut and immediately open them again, hoping the scar's movement is a work of my imagination. But no.

The damn thing is still pulsing, breathing, wiggling around.

What if it breaks through his skin and crawls on me? I shove his hand off my knee. "Don't touch me." I inch away from him as much as I can, hug my knees in tight to my chest. Sitting sandwiched between two Dusters doesn't allow me much elbow room, let alone room to slide away from either of them. I can feel their hunger pushing in on my personal space, trying to pop my bubble. But I need to make them think I'm one of them.

I clear my throat and say, "No disrespect, it's just one of my quirks—touching. You understand." I know he doesn't, but I say it anyway.

Realizing my shoulders are hiked up to my ears, I try to relax them. I kick out my legs to give the impression that I'm not scared. Well, I try to kick them out in a nonchalant way, but the movement is slow and choppy. One Converse falls off and I put it back on. Then I cross, uncross, and re-cross my ankles, trying not to let the shank show.

Damn it! Relax already. Breathe. In. Out.

There they go. My shoulders are hiked right up again. I reach behind and lean back on my hands, which naturally elevates my shoulders, but looks casual—I hope.

"How'd you hurt yourself?"

The question jars me. I don't know where it came from. My elbows weaken and I feel like I might collapse backwards.

How do they know?

"We could *smell* you before you even opened the door."

Shit! Are they in my head?

No. How's that even possible? I shake my head to clear my thinking as much as I can.

That voice. It's the same voice, and it sounds familiar, distant and warbly in my frantic mind, but familiar. I know I've heard it before.

I glance around the circle to see who it's coming from. Every face is staring at me, waiting. It appears as though the voice could have come from any one of them. But I believe it's from a man. If memory serves me right, it sounds like the voice I had once thought was the counselor. As I look from one man to the next, all around the group, I see one guy who is holding his upper arm. His hand is so scarred up I can't tell where one wound begins and the next one ends.

My voice is lodged in my throat. I don't know what to say. How the freaking holy Hell does he know? Even if they can actually smell the blood, how does he know where my wound is? And why isn't he also referring to his head, *my* head? If he knows about one, he *must* know about the other.

"You must be the counselor. What's your name? I was a bit too frazzled to get it on any of my previous visits to the group." I laugh, hoping it sounds genuine.

"Downright scared shitless is more like it, just like right now." He raises his thick, bushy eyebrows and stares at me intently. "My name's Clyde and I request that my patients don't hold *anything* back. So, how *did* you hurt yourself? We *all*," he glances around the circle and nods, "hope you're all right."

Everyone in the group nods in unison. It's a trance-like nodding, as though they're willed to do it all at once. Or like they are all part of one whole, multiple heads on the same monster.

"Scratching. Most of the time I don't even realize I'm doing it, not until I see the blood. It's a nervous tic."

"The bald spots. The bald spots. I told you." A few members to my left, I see a skinny girl backhanding the arm of the fat woman next to her—Renfield and Git Girl. "I told you it wasn't a fashion choice."

"I git it. I *git* it. Stop hitting me, Toodles. Jesus, you need to learn how to mellow."

"I knew it! Her face is much too pretty to want to have those bald spots. Though *she can* pull it off." Renfield, I mean Toodles —(That sick little minion doesn't even deserve a name.)—shoots me an apologetic look, chin down and crooked smile. "I mean, you, *you* could pull it off." She looks at Clyde and then back to me. "I know. Sorry. We must not talk about anyone in group as though they aren't here. We all forget that rule a lot. Sorry. Sorry."

Git Girl, who's sitting with her legs stretched out straight— since she is too fat to sit crossed legged— kicks her. She has to lean to the side in order to get her leg over far enough to reach Toodles's foot. Toodles, with her knees pulled in to her scrawny chest, topples to the side and falls against Medusa Man, the one with the scar worked into the Medusa tattoo on his shin.

"Sorry. Sorry. I didn't mean to. Sorry." Toodles immediately tries readjusting herself.

"No worries." A solemn gravelly voice comes from the Medusa Man, as he lightly grasps Toodles's arm and helps her get resettled and sit back up. He sounds like he's choking back tears, his voice squeezing up through restricted vocal chords.

"'*Sorry. Sorry.*' Toodles, you're such a people pleaser it's pathetic. Just stop, already. Geez." Git Girl rolls her eyes and inches away from Toodles as much as she can. She's now almost shoulder to shoulder with the guy sitting on her other side. I can't see his scar until he turns toward Git Girl and asks her to give him some space.

His cheekbone. Like Tommy, but bigger and longer and thicker. A job done, and redone, to completion, unlike Tommy's.

Why would anyone one of them want their scars so visible? It's like they want everyone to know who they are, *what* they are. Like they're proud of their actions. Almost showing off what they do. All except for…

Medusa Man. His is disguised, embedded in his tattoo. And the Fake Brit with his long sleeves.

Slug Man's voice bellows across the circle. "Why are you complaining, Sheila? After all, you're the one who nicknamed her Toodles." He mimics a female voice when he says, "'Come on over here and let me scrape those bones you skinny bitch.' Then when the job's done and you've had your fill, you wave her off and say 'Toodles,' then laugh." He mimics obnoxious tittering and reaches his hands out in front of himself, as though holding a fat belly that's jiggling from laughter. "Then you kick her in her scrawny ass as she's leaving and is *bleeding for you,* you fat inconsiderate cunt!"

Git Girl—Sheila—tries to stand up as she's yelling, "I'll cut you, too, you ugly, ign'ant fucker!"

Toodles touches Sheila's massive thigh and says, "Just ignore him, Shay-Shay. It's all right. I'll give you a fix after group. Just hold out. You don't need his dust." She smiles meekly. "Oh, and it's ig-nor-ant, not ign'ant."

Git Girl reels her head around and glares at her. That stare is so fierce it could bore holes into Toodles's skull. "Bitch, stop correcting me! You need to realize—two years as an Eng'ish major don't make you fucking Professa Know-It-All, and I *ain't* no student!"

"Yeah, well, by the sound of it, maybe you should be, you fat idiot!" someone yells out.

Git Girl stands up and kicks her pillow. Slug Man and Snake Girl part like the Red Sea and let it sail passed them and out of the now broken circle. Git Girl starts walking around the inner circle, staring down at every face she passes, while she repeats, "Who the fuck said that? You? You? You?"

Wow! I can't even believe what I'm hearing, what I'm seeing. This shit is messed up! I thought they were all in this together, one monster. I thought they were just after me, just non-junkie-cutters. Maybe I was wrong.

My knees are hugged in tight to my chest. My chin sits on

top. I feel the sweat soaking the bandana around my head. I'm fighting the intense urge to tear it off and start scratching. But I can't. I can't bleed in their presence. It's bad enough they already smell my wounds. I can't imagine how they'd react to me actually bleeding. Well, come to think of it, I can. That must be what triggered them to all come at me the first time I entered into this fucked-up group.

Git Girl is now standing in front of *me*. I look up at her with only my eyes, as she repeats, "You?"

I shake my head but never lift it off my knees. She hesitates, stares at me, then moves on.

I release the hold I have on my legs. I plant my hands firmly on the floor. Now more people are up on their feet. Defensive.

Offensive. You name it. The shit is ready to fly.

I look around. There isn't one single chair in the room. What the fuck am I supposed to use for a shield if she decides to come after me again? Or if they *all* do again? I look down at my seat—a cushy pillow.

Oh shit! What the Hell did I get myself into here?

I feel for the shank in my sock, wrapped in paper towels. But I don't dare pull it out. I'm outnumbered.

What was I thinking?

More people start yelling. So many voices are going at once that I can't make out much. Lots of "bitch, cunt, whore," and even more of, "I'll cut you." You get the picture. More pillows are kicked, thrown. It's a madhouse, madder than mad.

Scouting out the safest escape route, I ready myself to jump up and flee. Before I'm on my feet, someone grabs my arm, my good arm, and gives it a hard tug.

I'm getting dragged up off from my pillow seat. I get a strong whiff of body odor, before I'm able to turn and see Medusa Man with my arm in his massive mitt. He has a strong grip. For some odd reason the image of him turning wrenches under the hood of an old muscle car pops into my head. But why do I smell Fake Brit?

Then another hand grabs a hold of my other arm, my wound. I flinch.

"Sorry, love. But we have to move fast." He moves his hand off my wound and down to my elbow and keeps leading me, along with Medusa Man.

My feet are practically off the ground as the two Dusters pull me *into* the chaos. We're ducking and dodging and weaving in and out of the mass of pissed off junkie-cutters, flying pillows.

Damn it! I feel the shank has fallen out of my sock. We're almost at the door when a pillow knocks me upside the head. The bandana I'm wearing slides around and ends up pushed down over one of my eyes. I feel the cool air stinging my wounds.

Another pillow, then another, and another are smacking into us. I never imagined getting pelted with pillows would hurt, but when they're thrown with the intense anger of hungry, pissed off jonesing junkie-cutters they can hurt like a motherfucker. My wounds are throbbing. Fake Brit stumbles, lands on one knee, almost brings all three of us down. But Medusa Man reaches around me and gives him a hand.

We're almost at the door, almost free, when someone grabs what's left of my hair and yanks my head back.

I land on my back on the cold linoleum floor. Git Girl is standing over me, my hair still wrapped in her fat sausage fingers. The bandana is somehow still covering one of my eyes.

"Where do you think you're going, you skinny paranoid freak? I haven't dusted you yet!" Git Girl's only inches from my face. She's literally foaming from the mouth, and her spit lands in my one visible eye. Then she pulls off the bandana, leans down close, and licks my scabbed head. Her breath smells like a dirty ashtray and rotten eggs.

What's with all the fucking licking?

"That shit's never going down!" Medusa Man hollers, though it's not very loud, as his hammer of a fist punches Git Girl in the head. Once. Twice. And the third time finally knocks her on her fat ass.

Before I can attempt wiping the phlegm from my face, both of my arms are yanked, and I'm up on my feet again. The door is only a few feet away. Then, somehow over all the commotion, I hear, "I got this Freshie, Shay-Shay."

I look over my shoulder and see Toodles crouching down and picking up the shank from the floor. She then immediately looks up and glares at me. Before I can react, she's charging at me. She jumps over Git Girl, who's still on the floor and rubbing her head as though she doesn't know what just happened to her. Toodles's arm is outstretched, with the shank in her hand aimed right at me.

I turn away and duck my chin to my chest to protect my face. I don't think Fake Brit or Medusa Man know what's going on. I try to tell them, but I can't get the words out quick enough before I hear the nuthouse knife tear the back of my shirt. Then comes the white hot screaming pain as the blade slices down my shoulder blade. My back instantly arches and my head shoots up. A choked scream comes out of me.

Fake Brit turns to see Toodles, shank in hand, raising her hand up for another slice. He swings his arm back and clips her in the face with his elbow. She stumbles back, holding her instantly bloody nose, and lands on Git Girl. I turn back to the door. I hear the two Dusters wrestling around, and Git Girl is yelling obscenities.

Fake Brit lets out a strained laugh, then reaches for the door-knob. The knob doesn't turn. He tries again. Nothing.

Medusa Man slides the stringless cloth blind aside, the one that's pulled down over the door's window. I see red hair.

"What the fuck?" He says and then—

He slides the blind up, revealing Nurse Hatchet, and that creepy-chipper Cheshire grin, on the other side holding the doorknob.

A fist flies past my face. The mesh-filled window crackles and spiderwebs.

She doesn't flinch. She actually moves a little closer and puts a second hand on the doorknob.

I knew it! Well, I didn't suspect *she* was the one in-the-know, but I figured *someone* had to be, someone besides the counselor —Clyde. How else could this shit fly under the radar, unless someone on staff was helping hide the secrets of these Duster monsters? I'd actually suspected Dick, the David Coverdale wannabe, was in cahoots with the counselor. But she makes more sense, inconspicuous and all. The picture of innocence. Dick is just ignorant and ruled by the wrong head.

Medusa Man pulls his hand back and punches again. More crackling, more spiderwebbing.

She still stands unflinching, her mischievous Cheshire grin beaming.

Why does she have to ruin the Cheshire for me?

"Bloody Hell! It's not going through. You're only hurting yourself," says Fake Brit.

One more punch from Medusa Man sends the window bowing out toward the hallway. Nurse Hatchet steps back. Her grip on the doorknob slips free.

Before I know what's happening, we're out in the hallway. Hatchet gets a kick in the gut from Medusa Man's slippered foot, and she's thrown back into the wall.

The first responder: Tommy. Diagonally across the hall from the Group Counseling Room, he has the cleaning cart strategically positioned between the exit from behind the staff desk and the door to the nurse's station.

"Damn, that was fast," he says to us as he kicks over his mop bucket of soapy water before rushing to our sides. The ring full of room keys is unlatched from his belt loop and in his hand when…

CHAPTER 14

Tommy gets in front of the three of us and leads us down the long hallway of patient rooms. I'm trying to run *with* everyone, but my feet are barely touching the floor. Fake Brit and Medusa Man still have a hold of me.

I shake and shimmy in their grasp as I say, "Let me go. We'll run faster." I hear sloshing and stumbling and indistinct chatter coming from behind us.

The guys give a quick glance over their shoulders, and then they each release their grasp on me. We pick up speed. I assume Tommy is leading us to the small Common Room at the end of the hall. It's directly across from Git Girl's room, and I bet those monsters would never think we'd go near there. But we end up standing breathless in front of the door that punctuates the end of the hall. The one I've never seen anyone use. The one that's always locked.

Tommy's fumbling with his excess of keys, trying to find the right one, before he comes to one that's oddly shaped. It's one of three skeleton keys on the ring.

Why would such an old looking key unlock a modern style door?

The key grinds in the key hole. It won't go all the way in. He pulls it out and reinserts it. A breath later, I hear that magical *click* sound. Tommy pushes down on the door handle and we escape through to the other side.

We're now standing on a landing of a dark and winding stairwell. Lights above us and below us are flickering, threatening to illuminate us, like a lighthouse beckoning the way for others to find us. The small square window in the door is too high up for me to clearly see through, and it is so dingy it almost looks like it's tinted. But there are smudges in the grime.

Tommy ushers us past him and down the stairs. He holds up, backtracks a few steps, and peers through the door's window. Medusa Man and Fake Brit thunder down the stairs. I'm on their heels for a handful of steps, but then I hesitate and look back for Tommy. I can't see him or the door we just came through.

A couple seconds pass, then I hear him say, "Shit! Rick." He leans over the railing and whisper-yells, "They're after us. Go. Go!" Then he's blazing down the stairs toward me.

I turn and bolt, taking two steps at a time. I can't help but laugh to myself—I hear Tommy's voice in my head, *"Shit Dick."* I can't help but hear it that way.

What is wrong with me? This is no time for laughter.

Something trips me up. I stumble down a couple steps. I grab the old metal railing and catch myself. I look down. The steps are crumbling. The lower we descend, the worse the crumbling gets. The steps are covered with linoleum flooring, black and white checkerboard that's extremely worn and faded, and each step is seemed at the edge with metal stripping. The linoleum is cracked and peeling. The stripping is coming unstuck and sticking out here and there. And the stairs are actually falling apart.

Now steady on my feet, I take another step down and the stair starts cracking, threatening to crumble under my weight. I move faster down the stairs, hoping the speed will keep things intact. No matter how fast I go, if I step too close to the edge of any stair, it starts to break away.

How is this area not blocked off from *anyone* coming in here? It's obviously an OSHA violation.

As best I can, I keep to the middle of the steps as I descend farther down the stairwell. I've lost sight of Medusa Man and Fake Brit, but I can hear them ahead of me—thudding as they jump steps, and cursing. The stairs must be falling apart under them, too. I pay closer attention to the steps as I go and notice— yes, some are already broken when I get to them.

Tommy is on my tail. I hear his footfalls right behind me, along with his grunts and his cursing our crumbling escape route.

The lights above each landing are still flickering, at least the ones that work at all. There are a couple landings that are so dimly lit I don't want to let go of the railing for fear the layout may all of a sudden change. And it does. Though I don't realize this until—

I hear thuds and stumbling only seconds before I hear "What the fuck?"

I don't stop. Tommy is right at my ass. A moment later, I trip and hit the floor hard.

Then Tommy stumbles over something, then stumbles over me and hits the floor harder.

I look up and try to figure out what just happened. It's dark, but I can make out the shapes of all of us in a jumbled mess on the floor and the flickering stairwell looming above us. The shank-slice on my back is screaming. We're all fidgeting and trying to get out from under one another, as huffs and grunts and curses escape us. Then all at once we're all shushing each other.

All movement and sound ceases. Well, all sound except for the crackling of the faulty lighting. I hadn't noticed that noise when we first rushed into the stairwell. But now, as we're all lying here on the floor listening intently, the sound is so eerie that I never would have come in here in the first place had I not been running for my life.

The seconds tick by at the pace of a five-legged spider on its death-crawl. All of us cast a questioning glance from one person to the next, over and over a few times until Medusa Man quietly asks, "Where the fuck do we go now?"

Tommy straightens himself up and sits with his back against the wall. We all follow his lead. Then Tommy speaks up. He talks in a low voice, almost a whisper. "Well, we haven't heard any doors open, so I think it's safe to say they don't know we escaped into the stairwell. I think we should hunker down here for a short time. Everyone will be looking for us on the outside —in the wards and outside the hospital." Reaching down to his lap, he grasps the ring full of keys, careful not to jingle them, and fans them out on the palm of his hand. "I can get us through this door," he motions with a head nod toward the door Fake Brit is unconsciously leaning against, "and into the basement of the old wing. But, like I said, they'll be looking for us for a while. So we should wait here until we think the search has died…down."

I'm unaware why he paused just then, until an instant later I see a light flash through the window high above Fake Brit's head, through the window I didn't realize was there, on the door we were *just told* was there. All of us instantly, successively, hug our legs in close to our chests. The image reminds me of fingers curling in a drumming-like fashion toward the palm of the hand to make a fist. The beam of light slowly moves up the stairs and back down, until finally landing only inches in front of Medusa Man's baby-blue-slippered feet. The ray of illumination forms a distorted circle on the crumbled linoleum floor. Medusa Man stays stone still and stares. I don't think he's even breathing. Come to think of it, I don't think *any* of us are breathing.

A *slide-clink* sounds out, metal on metal. A key in the keyhole of the door.

I suck in air through my nose, an almost silent gasp. My shoulders hike up to my ears. I squeeze my legs in tighter. The tension in my muscles reminds me of stepping out from a woodstove heated cabin into a below-zero blizzard.

My fresh wound stings and throbs. I can feel my back slightly slipping and sliding against the wall. Blood. I hope I don't need stitches.

The distorted circle of light starts moving spastically around the floor. Unable to blink, I just stare and wait.

One of Medusa Man's feet is illuminated—once, twice, three times until…

A high pitched electric whir rings out from somewhere up the stairs. One of the lights a couple landings up flickers, threatening to either go to black or light up our hiding nook. The *whirring* remains constant, and the landing light is suspended in a sort of limbo—somewhere between light and dark.

Medusa Man's foot is lit up a fourth time. His jaw tightens as he clenches his teeth. I can hear his teeth grinding. A moment later, the circle-ish light snaps out, followed by another metallic *slide-clink*. From under the door comes a *clankety-clanking* sound, like a ring of keys falling on the floor. A muffled voice, then a second voice, and possibly a third. A conversation. I can't make out any words. All of us start glancing back and forth at one another. Fake Brit turns his head to the side, putting his ear flush against the metal door. The rest of us watch him intently.

The voices from the other side fade away. Fake Brit turns back toward us and shrugs.

The electric whir coming from up the stairwell fizzles and crackles, then dies away. The dim limbo-light is snuffed out. All is dark and dead silent.

CHAPTER 15

Minutes pass. I don't know how many. Time feels stagnant. I still don't dare to budge. None of us move.

Then, all at once, we release our breath. It comes out as one heavy, unified sigh.

In an instant I realize my nose is smothered with the stench of body odor.

"Seriously, a shower. Ever heard of it?" The blatant insult tastes unpleasant on my lips. I cup my nose, then nudge the Fake Brit with my elbow. "I don't mean to sound mean, but the smell is overpowering." I can't believe I just voluntarily touched a stranger *and* am trying to joke with him. It must be the whole saving-my-ass-from-Dusters-thing that makes me less anxious in the company I'm with. Who knows?

"Hey, love, I shower. Three times a week. Any more than that is obsessive. Huh, Americans." I feel him raise his arm. He sniffs a loud exaggerated sniff. "I'm not that manky." He sniffs again. "Well, maybe it's the all-natural deodorant stone I use."

"No, that shit's straight up b.o.. That stone does *not* work. And who are you kidding? *You're* a fucking American, too.

We're not dumb. Your fake accent sucks." Medusa Man fidgets, then adds, "No offense. I just call it like I see it. Ha! Or smell it."

I want to laugh, but I still don't understand what these two Dusters are doing hiding out with us. "So, what *gives*? Why did you two run from your Duster group anyway, *and* help *me* escape? I don't understand any of this crazy-ass shit. Someone please explain what the Hell is going on here."

All is silent for a moment. I look from Medusa Man to the Fake Brit. Then they look at one another. Neither of them says a word.

I huff and plop my head down on my bent knees, hiding my face. "Please, someone, *anyone,* enlighten us already."

Someone takes a deep breath, and it all starts spilling out.

"Yeah, we're junkie-cutters, or Dusters as *you* call us. But Davey and I only cut *ourselves*, only use *our own* bone dust to get high. By the way," Medusa Man nudges me with his elbow, "that's a cool name. Dusters. I *like* it." He smiles at me, but his smile quickly slips from his face as he tells us, "All those other crazy fuckers in group, well, they're all just…crazy fuckers." He laughs, though it sounds like uncomfortable, nervous laughter forcing its way out.

"Davey. Okay, good. Now I can stop calling you Fake Brit in my head." I laugh this time, real laughter. Medusa Man and Tommy join in.

"*See*, I told you—you weren't fooling *any* of us with that *lousy* accent." Medusa Man playfully kicks Davey's slippered foot.

Good, I've lightened the mood, at least for a moment. Though that wasn't my intention. Nerves—sometime things just fly out of my mouth without forethought.

"Okay, okay. Now let's back up. So, not *all* Dusters dust *other* people? I don't understand *any* of this." Tommy sits up straighter and looks at the two Dusters intently.

Medusa Man looks at Davey. They both nod.

"Well, I'm quite shattered, and since my so-called *fake* accent annoys everyone so much, why don't you go ahead and fill them in, Shawn."

Medusa Man—Shawn—continues his story. "Long-time bone dust users start getting all crazy. The longer you use the crazier you get. It fucks with your brain chemistry somehow. I don't know all the technicalities and medical mumbo-jumbo, but long-time use turns people into sadists. They *actually get off* on dusting other people. *Sick fuckers* is what they are." He fidgets and then continues. "Davey and I are here trying to get clean, *seriously* trying, before *we* turn into *them*. Those other Dusters are here for more sinister reasons. Oh…and their *senses*. Once they've dusted someone else, especially a Freshie— someone who has *never* been dusted (And I hear a Freshie's dust gives the most intense high.)—somehow they develop these superhuman senses. Once that happens, the switch is flipped and there's no coming back. It's some creepy ass shit."

"Like smelling my wounds before I was in the room?"

Shawn nods. "Just like dogs after their first taste of blood."

"Or vampires," adds Davey.

Shawn kicks Davey's foot. "Don't be lame."

Davey just shrugs.

"I don't know about Davey here, but once I started feeling the temptation to dust others, I signed myself in here. The pull is freakishly strong, and I came close once, but . . . I don't know. It's one thing to harm myself to get a free high, but to harm someone else . . . well, I can't let it go *that* far." Shawn's crackly, strained voice sounds close to tears.

"Same," Davey says. "I came close *more* than once, and both times it was someone I care for very much. If I'd given in, I would be absolutely gutted and would never forgive myself."

"What about Clyde, the counselor? What's *his* deal? He

allows all of this to go on?" As I'm asking this, Tommy gently stops my hand from scratching my head. Why don't *I* realize I'm doing this?

"Clyde's just another *sick fucker*, as Shawn so eloquently put it." Davey says. "He's just downright smarmy. We've been filing complaints about that dodgy group for the past couple of weeks, requesting a new counselor, since Clyde is obviously mad as a bag of ferrets. But that flaming ginger bitch is the one who took our forms, so it looks like no one else has a *clue* what's what. I don't know." He shakes his head. "It's all cocked-up is what it is."

The electric whir sounds up again, and the landing light up the stairs lights up full glare. We all hush and freeze, staring up at the light. Out of my peripheral I see Tommy's hand is resting on his bent knee and clutching his key ring. The three ancient-looking skeleton keys stand out among all the rest of the shiny silver ones.

After a few agonizing moments, the landing light starts buzzing and flickering, again. I let out my breath that I didn't realize I was holding in.

"What's with the old creepy skeleton keys? This wing doesn't seem *that* old, especially from the looks of these doors." I run my finger across the keys, making them jingle and sway. "And why do *you*, a *janitor*, have keys to a wing you don't work in?"

"I double as extra hands for the maintenance crew. They had the keys for this wing made to look like old skeleton keys so that they'd be easy to find on our overflowing key-ring. It was all supposed to be a kind of joke. There are rumors of the sick, disturbing practices that went on in this wing when it was up and running back in the day. And that comes with more talk— talk of hauntings from past abused patients. All rumors, of course."

"Of course," I say.

All goes silent again. Every one of us fidgets, readjusting our positions. The landing light silently snuffs out. Total darkness engulfs us.

CHAPTER 16

Before any of us hear a sound, the door at our backs slides open. Davey and I fall backwards. The shank slice from Toodles screams. I reflexively arch my back and squeeze my eyes shut.

"What the fuck?" I hear Shawn's strained voice. Then shuffling feet.

Someone is gently pulling on my non-injured arm, trying to sit me up. I open my eyes and see dark chocolate eyes peering at me through a curtain of long dread locks.

"Sunshine? How'd you know where . . ." Tommy's voice trips up in his throat. "Wait. What's *he* doing with you? What's going on?"

Behind Irie is Rick, the David Coverdale wannabe douche who chased us down, but *somehow* lost us. I stand beside Irie. I'm leery about *Dick*.

"He's cool. He's with me—with us." Irie pats Rick on the back. "I've filled him in on the deal with the Dusters. And…"

"I've been wondering about that weird NA group for a while, but that Nurse Hatchet has a Medusa stare. She always manages to jumble my thoughts right when I think I'm figuring this crazy shit out. I get all weak in the knees and freeze up when she's around. And she *always* seems to be around. Even when I think it's not her shift, she just magically appears. What's *her deal* anyway? Is she a, ah, what do you call them? Dusters?"

"We're trying to figure *that* one out." Tommy stands up, straightens his clothes, and clips his key ring to a belt loop on his Dickies.

Now Davey stands up. "Shawn and I have been filing complaint reports with her about that group. It's been two weeks since the first report, but nothing has been done. So it seems like..."

"She held the fucking door shut! She wouldn't let us out! There's no *'seems like'* about it. She's in on all this psycho shit. She's probably a Duster-whore, like Toodles." Shawn's eloquence scrapes up out of his vocal chords. Every time he talks, the veins in his neck pop out, looking like a tangle of rivers.

"Aren't *you* two Dusters, too?" Rick takes a couple steps back. "Why are you guys here with *these* two?" He points at Tommy and me with his thumb.

Davey fills him in, as Tommy and Irie hug. "Thank you, Baby Girl. Thank you."

"Dad, there are others on the staff that I told about the Dusters. They called me in when they couldn't find you. They wanted to fire you. They thought you were trying to help patients escape. So I told them. I told them everything—I told them about Mom."

After ten or so minutes of various conversations, all going on at once, the six of us head back up to the third floor. It turns out that the psychiatrist for the adult unit, Dr. Headstrom, the one I *still* haven't met yet, is one of the people on staff that Irie had a lengthy conversation with about the Dusters and what the worst ones are capable of. He said he was going to call in the authorities. But he told Irie that we will first need evidence before *anyone* will even *consider* our claims.

Here comes the next crazy plan I can't believe I go along with.

CHAPTER 17

It's a set-up. With me as bait.

I'm going to be *completely* bald by the time I get out of this psycho hospital.

It's almost three in the morning. I've been counting the second *ticks* and the hour *clicks* on the wall clock. I want to sleep, but there's *no* way in Hell *that's* going to happen. My nerves won't allow it. Plus, the plan...

Sheila wants so desperately to dust me—a Freshie— that we figure this will be the best way to lure them out, get them to let their guard down, reveal themselves for who they really are— evil sadists.

It's completely dark in my room. The door is closed.

Wait.

Maybe that's why they haven't tried to dust me yet. The door to my room hasn't been closed since I was first admitted here.

I jump out of bed and ease the door open just a little. Rick is at his post outside my room. His chin is resting on his chest, as he pretend-sleeps. He's even pretend-snoring.

He *better* be pretending!

I wonder if he should be there at all. Maybe we should've had him somewhere down the hall flirting with Nurse Hatchet. That would be more realistic.

No. Rick's hard-on wouldn't have allowed him to think straight. Better he's here watching over me, rather than with Nurse Hatchet's tits staring him in the face.

A sliver of light slices across my midsection as I'm lying in bed again. Maybe I should open the door wider. I don't know. This whole plan has me right on edge. Now I'm *well aware* that I can't stop scratching. The sheet under my head is all smeared in blood.

Stop. Stop. Stop! I *want* hair. I *really* do.

I roll over and face the wall. The Dusters may be more apt to approach me if I'm turned away from them. I readjust my blanket and shirt just right.

Tick-tick-tick-tick-tick, click. Three AM on the dot and I hear a brief fluttering sound, like a flag whipping in the wind. As soon as it stops, I feel someone looking at me.

A second later—I feel someone standing close, right behind me.

But I never heard footsteps.

And why is there no shadow?

My breath gets stuck. My heart rate skips a couple beats, like a dirty needle on a vinyl record, then it speeds up. It's thumping so fast and so hard it feels like the blanket on me must be moving. I've strategically allowed the fresh wound on my back to be uncovered. The shirt I had on when Toodles sliced me open is what I'm wearing, as planned. Our hopes are that the smell of blood, open flesh, will lure at least one of them. I'm not sure if that's what did it, but *someone* is in my room. I can feel their presence.

But I can't hear them breathing.

I hope like Hell it's Sheila, that fat psycho cunt.

Tick-tick-tick-tick-tick

Why hasn't she tried anything yet? Is she just watching me sleep? What gives?

Tick-tick-tick

The sliver of light from the open door widens. I hear feet shuffling. Ragged breathing. A shadow. A large one. And it's getting bigger, closer.

Now there are two of them in my room. Why did they come separate? Maybe Toodles came in first to make sure I was asleep? But I wouldn't think she'd dare do any such thing without Sheila at her side. Plus, where *is* the first one? I only see one shadow.

Wait.

The shadow stopped. They've turned their head away from me. I hear whispers.

But I thought the first person was right behind me, too? Where are they now? It looks like the shadow's head is turned toward the bathroom door in the far corner of the room. What is going on?

The anticipation of the attack is killing me. I may die of a heart attack before any attempted dusting even happens.

Silence.

The shadow's looking at me again. And it's moving. And growing.

I can't breathe. I have to find my breath. I need to follow through with the plan.

The light from the door is snuffed almost completely out by the enormous shadow right behind me. Shallow, ragged breathing.

They're nervous? Or Sheila's just out of breath from carrying her own heft down the hall.

I'm ready. My breath found me. I can do this—I think.

The shadow shifts. A piece of it is slowly rising. Higher. Higher. Then it freezes.

I flip around, hold up a camera, and hold down the button. Multiple flashes light up the room like a disco ball, as a myriad of successive pictures snap rapidly.

I'm seeing double, triple. The flashes are blinding. The person of the shadow freezes, covering their eyes with their weapon-free hand. Then, in my peripheral, I see Nurse Hatchet. She's in the far corner of the room near the bathroom. She's just standing there watching, Cheshire smile almost glowing. Red tendrils of hair shining, almost flaming, and flowing as though windblown.

A flash later she's gone.

Then the door flies open so fast the doorknob slams into the wall.

"Lights, camera…"

"Action."

The overhead light is blaring. I see Davey holding up an iPhone as though it's a gun and he's taken aim. Shawn is wielding something large over his head, ready to pummel my attacker. And Tommy is front and center, mop handle in hand, and he starts swinging.

"What the fuck is go…" My attacker ducks their head and starts waving their arms to block the blows from Tommy. I hear what must be the shank clatter onto the floor.

Shawn throws whatever it is he brought as a weapon. It hits the intruder with a dull thud.

My attacker, holding their midsection, hits the floor with an even louder thud.

Before I can swing my legs over the edge of the bed to stand up, all three of my guard dogs are on top of the sick fuck who tried to dust me. Fists are flying. Thuds, smacks, and cries of pain sound out.

"Stop. We've got them. Stop." I don't recognize this voice.

A tall, wiry man is standing in the doorway. He's wearing a dark gray suit and a white coat.

Tommy, Davey, and Shawn let up on my attacker and jump to their feet.

"Dr. Headstrom. Sorry. Heat of the moment and all." Tommy is straitening his ponytail, tucking loose strands of hair behind his ear.

Sheila is curled up in the fetal position beside my bed, moaning and cursing. The shank is lying on the floor next to her. An oversized ottoman is lying on the floor in front of the bathroom.

"*Shawn!* You brought an *ottoman* as a *weapon?*"

He shrugs. "What? It's heavy. And it worked didn't it?" He smirks.

Davey puts his arm around Shawn's shoulders and laughs. "And it took the bitch down. Bloody genius!"

I look around, confused. "Where's Rick? He should've been the first person to respond. And the nurse. Did anyone see her leave?"

Dr. Headstrom is now kneeling down next to Sheila, who is groaning in pain. "Rick's still outside your door."

Tommy steps over to the doorway and glances around the corner. "He's sleeping?" He looks back at us, confusion written all over his face. Turning back to Rick, Tommy reaches out and shakes his shoulder, "Rick. Rick. You were only supposed to *pretend* to sleep. Rick!" He shakes him harder this time.

A thud.

I see Rick, arm outstretched over his head as he's now lying on the floor—still dead asleep.

Tommy steps out of sight. A paper coffee cup rolls in front of the door. Then Tommy is back in view. "You'd think *that* would have kept him awake."

Tommy and I look at each other, an aha-moment. Instantly we both know what the other is thinking. At the same time both of us say, "Drugged?"

Tommy immediately crouches next to Rick and feels for a pulse. His wrist. His neck. The look he throws back into the room is one of panic, tight-lipped and bug-eyed. Then he leans down close to Rick's face, feeling for breath. Tommy's shoulders drop. "He's breathing. But I couldn't find his pulse." He starts reaching for the coffee cup.

"Don't touch it!" Shawn rushes to the doorway, holding out his hand in a stop gesture.

Tommy's arm recoils. "Shit! Thanks Shawn." He looks back in at each of us, from one face to the next and back to Rick. "What the Hell is going on here?"

Dr. Headstrom, still crouched next to Sheila, looks over at me. "You asked about a nurse. Did you see one?"

"Yes. Right before Sheila… I never heard her come in, but I saw her. When the flashes were going off. She was right over there." I turn and point to the far corner of the room next to the bathroom. "One second she was there. The next gone. Like she just vanished or something. Did any of you see her leave?"

I look around at all the faces in my room.

Laughter. But no one I'm looking at is smiling, not even a hint of a smile.

We all turn at the same time and look at Sheila. She's rolled over on her back, still holding her midsection, laughing maniacally. Her hands bounce with every laughing-jiggle of her massive stomach. "You'll only see her when she wants you to see her."

"Nurse who?" Dr. Headstrom stands up, pushes his wire-framed glasses up his nose, and looks around at each of us.

"Hatchet. Nurse Hatchet. The redhead hotty that poor Rick here is always flirting with." Tommy pats Rick on the back.

Then a more worried look washes over his face, and he leans down again to make sure Rick is still breathing. "Phew. Still with us. But we *really* need to make a call. *Now.*"

As he slowly walks to the door, Dr. Headstrom pulls his cell phone out of his jacket pocket. Before he dials 911, he says, "Hatchet, you say?" He looks at Tommy, who nods.

Dr. Headstrom shakes his head. "There is no Nurse Hatchet. Not on *my* staff. Is she from another unit?"

Tommy, Davey, Shawn, and I pass looks of bafflement from one to the other.

Sheila's laughter hits a mind-grating volume, as she bounds up off the floor and lunges, shank in hand, at me.

CHAPTER 18

WHEN THE POLICE ARRIVE, Sheila's still in a four-point restraint on my bedroom floor. Tommy, Davey, Shawn, and Dr. Headstrom are sweat-drenched and exhausted. The cuffs are slapped on her immediately after the two officers come into the room.

Back against the wall, knees hugged in tight, I'm still shaking on the bed. I'm just as sweaty as the guys are. I escaped another Duster attack. Someone please cuff me, too. I want so badly to scratch the Hell out of myself. I don't think I can restrain any longer.

Later, in the Common Room, after all police statements have been filled out, all questioning completed, the four of us—Tommy, Shawn, Davey, and myself—sit in a strained silence around the card table, door closed. The ticks of the wall-clock seem to echo around the room.

Hands on the table, fingers laced together, chin resting on top, I stare at the door with no idea what to say. Thoughts are swirling, like a tornado. I can't grasp any of them. My fingers twitch. I want to scratch. But I refuse to give in. Then the doorknob turns. The door clicks open. I jump up out of my chair. The chair falls backwards, clattering on the floor.

Dr. Headstrom walks in and I can breathe again. "They say Rick's going to make it, *and* they've arrested Sheila. But no others. The police need to investigate the NA group—the Dusters, as you all call them—before determining whether any of them are guilty of the things they've been accused of." He picks up my chair and sits at the table. Beside him, I remain standing.

"At least we got one of them," says Shawn.

Tommy immediately jumps in. "Yeah, but now the rest of them are going to be on a rampage."

"But with investigating eyes on them," I add.

"So, Dory, if you're not an addict, *or* a Duster, why were you in that group at all?" Dr. Headstrom looks confused.

"That's where I was *told* to go. Dropped off at the door *every* time."

"By who?"

I look at Tommy and the guys. "Nurse Hatchet." I grasp the table's edge, refusing to allow any scratching.

A tight-lipped Dr. Headstrom nods, then reaches into his coat pocket and pulls out the camera. He slides it to the center of the table. He doesn't look at any of us. He just stares at the camera as he says, "They've looked at all the images, down-loaded copies to a USB drive . . . There's no Nurse Hatchet, but there's something . . . something odd in the pictures."

The rest of us throw confused looks around the table. Shawn is the first to reach out and clutch the camera. It makes a drawn-out dinging sound as he turns it on. He clicks through the pictures. Then he freezes. Stares. Slowly, hesitantly, he hands the camera to Davey. He sucks in a deep breath and holds it, as he hands it to Tommy. Tommy does the exact same thing, and hands it to me.

The image on the screen: Sheila is shrouded in a black

swirling mist, though you can make out that it's her by her shape and her size and her clothes.

The hand.

Behind her raised, shank-wielding hand is a large outstretched swath of red in the vague shape of wings. In the center, between the wings and just above Sheila's hand, is the smokey image of a skull, barely visible but there. The eyes are glowing red, like flames. A second later, those red eyes flicker.

I gasp. The camera hits the floor. It doesn't break.

Dr. Headstrom looks at me, then we both look down at the camera. The image is still visible. The eyes are still flickering.

"You see that, right?" I say to the doctor.

Dr. Headstrom doesn't say a word, only nods. Then the image disappears. The camera clicks off.

It's all gone black.

ABOUT THE AUTHOR

Renee S. DeCamillis is the author of the psychological thriller/supernatural horror/bizarro novella The Bone Cutters. Renee is currently a horror novel editor for Wicked House Publishing, and she is a former Editorial Intern for the 5-time Bram Stoker award-winning speculative fiction and dark fiction publisher Crystal Lake Publishing. She is a member of the Horror Writers Association, the New England Horror Writers, and the Horror Writers of Maine. Renee is also a singer/songwriter/guitarist, the lead singer and rhythm guitarist for the band Scars Aligned, & a tree-hugging hippie with a sharp metal edge.

Renee's short fiction appears in the After the Burn post-apocalyptic anthology from Rogue Owl Press; the Wicked Women anthology from NEHW Press; Northern Frights: The Journal of Horror Writers of Maine Vol. 2.5 Lost; Deadman's Tome: The Conspiracy Issue; Siren's Call eZine Issue 37 the 6th Annual Women In Horror Month Edition, The Other Stories Podcast. Her poetry appears in The Horror Writers Association Poetry Showcase Volume IV.

Renee earned her BA in psychology from the University of Southern Maine, her MFA in Popular Fiction Writing from the Stonecoast Graduate Program, and she attended Berklee

College of Music as a music business major with guitar as her principal instrument. Renee is a former model, school rock band teacher, creative writing teacher, private guitar instructor, A&R rep for an indie record label, therapeutic mentor, psychological technician, and preschool teacher. She is also a former gravedigger; she can get rid of a body fast without leaving a trace, and she is not afraid of getting her hands dirty. Renee lives in the woods of Maine with her husband, their son, and a house full of ghosts.